"To a successful partnership."

She tilted her glass in a mocking salute. "So confident."

"I don't intend to lose, Quinn."

"Then let the best candidate win."

Her green gaze glittered as she lifted her glass and swirled its dark contents around the edge. She closed her eyes and breathed the wine in. Matteo found himself hypnotized by the way she gave herself over to the full sensual experience. Quinn Davis was *definitely* scorching hot on the inside. The type who would be more than a match for any man.

The question was, did she ever drop that rigid exterior and let herself go? Stretch out like a cat and let a man pleasure her until she screamed?

She opened her eyes. Looked directly into his. He was not nearly quick enough to wipe the curiosity off his face. A rosy hue stole over her golden skin; her gaze dropped away from his.

He could work with this.

Jennifer Hayward has been a fan of romance and adventure since filching her sister's Harlequin Mills & Boon® novels to escape her teenage angst.

Jennifer penned her first romance at nineteen. When it was rejected, she bristled at her mother's suggestion that she needed more life experience. She went on to complete a journalism degree before settling into a career in public relations. Years of working alongside powerful, charismatic CEOs and travelling the world provided perfect fodder for the arrogant alpha males she loves to write about—and free research on some of the world's most glamorous locales.

With a suitable amount of life experience under her belt, she sat down and conjured up the sexiest, most delicious Italian wine magnate she could imagine, had him make his biggest mistake and gave him a wife on the run. That story, THE DIVORCE PARTY, won her Harlequin's *So You Think You Can Write* contest and a book contract. Turns out Mother knew best.

With the first item on her bucket list complete, Jennifer is working her way through the rest. She put #2 in the bag when she talked her way into the jumpseat of an Airbus for landing on a flight from San Jose to Toronto, complete with headphones and a flight plan. The only thing missing was a follow-up date with the Robert Redford lookalike pilot. Figuring that #3—walking the runway as an angel at the Victoria's Secret Christmas fashion show—is not likely to happen, she's concentrating on #4 and #5, which are touring Australia and building a dream beach house in Barbados.

A native of Canada's gorgeous East coast, Jennifer now lives in Toronto with her Viking husband and their young Viking-in-training. She considers her ten-year-old-strong bookclub, comprised of some of the most amazing women she's ever met, a sacrosanct date in her calendar. And some day they will have their monthly meeting at her fantasy beach house, waves lapping at their feet, wine glasses in hand.

You can find Jennifer on Facebook and Twitter.

Recent titles by the same author:

AN EXQUISITE CHALLENGE
THE DIVORCE PARTY

THE TRUTH
ABOUT DE CAMPO

BY
JENNIFER HAYWARD

Published in Great Britain 2014
by Mills & Boon, an imprint of Harlequin (UK) Limited,
Eton House, 18-24 Paradise Road, Richmond, Surrey, TW9 1SR

© 2014 Jennifer Drogell

ISBN: 978 0 263 24220 1

Harlequin (UK) Limited's policy is to use papers that are natural,
renewable and recyclable products and made from wood grown in
sustainable forests. The logging and manufacturing processes conform
to the legal environmental regulations of the country of origin.

Printed and bound in Great Britain
by CPI Antony Rowe, Chippenham, Wiltshire

THE TRUTH ABOUT DE CAMPO

For two of my great inspirations:

My family—my anchor in this journey we call life.

And my bookclub girls who inspire me to write rum punch promises in the sand...and keep them!

RPP Forever.

CHAPTER ONE

Unless Matteo De Campo was mistaken, this conversation with his brother had all the hallmarks of a classic intervention.

It *looked* like it with Riccardo staring him down like a Spanish bullfighter with his eye on the unruly target. It *sounded* like it from his cautionary, bordering-on-aggressive tone. And it certainly *felt* like it with the De Campo CEO's displeasure licking over his skin like a flame.

If the truth be known, it had always been that way. They were like night and day, he and his brother. Where Riccardo was dark and intense and bulldozed his way through life, Matteo preferred the subtle approach. Both in business and in bed. You could catch more flies with honey. Persuade more effectively with a sophisticated argument than a head-on tackle.

Entice a woman into bed with a carefully timed observation that showed you *had* been listening to her over that bottle of Chianti.

He brought his gaze back to his brother's dark face. From the looks of it, Riccardo thought he was doing a bit *too* much of that these days.

Flicking an imaginary speck of dust off his suit, he lounged back against the floor-to-ceiling windows of his brother's Wall Street office and cocked a brow. "So what you're saying is *your* behavior was perfectly acceptable, but mine is not?"

"No," Riccardo emitted coolly. "What I'm saying is I don't know what in *Cristo's* name is wrong with you. You're treating the women of this planet like they're your own personal wrecking yard."

Matteo shrugged. "Maybe I've decided your way is the better way."

Riccardo shot him an amused look. "You forget I'm a reformed man. Happily married and loving it."

"Only because you met a goddess who's willing to put up with you," he muttered, digging his hands in his pockets and giving his head a restless shake. "Did you really ask me here to discuss my love life, Ric? Somehow I think you're much too busy for that."

"You're the vice president of sales and marketing for De Campo, Matty. Your love life *is* my business when it starts disrupting things around here."

"And *how*," Matteo drawled, "do you figure it's doing that?"

"Your antics in the tabloids are making it impossible for you or anyone else in this company to concentrate. Alex is tired of doing damage control, and frankly, I don't blame her."

Ebbene, so that stung. Matteo liked his sister-in-law. Didn't like the thought of making more work for her when she already worked far too much. But he was too irritated by his brother's rebuke not to strike back. "If I made the cover every week for the rest of the year I still wouldn't beat your record."

"*Si,* but I'm a better multitasker," Riccardo taunted.

Matteo stiffened, straightening away from the windows and eating up the distance between him and his brother with long furious strides. "I am making a *mockery* of my predecessor's numbers."

"Exactly why I want you to straighten yourself out. Think what you can do with a clear head."

Matteo could have told Riccardo he was definitely planning on doing that. That he'd sworn off women like an alcoholic swears off drink, potentially for the rest of his life given his recent spat of disastrous assignations. But he liked to yank Riccardo's chain as much as his brother liked to yank his. "What are you going to do if I don't?" he queried, leveling his gaze on his brother's angular, unforgiving face. "Punish me? Send me off to sell wine to the devout?"

Riccardo's coal-black eyes flashed. "As much as I would dearly love to have you out of the picture right now, I need you. And I think *you* need a challenge. Badly."

Matteo couldn't deny the truth of that statement. He'd almost doubled sales as head of De Campo's European operations. Was killing it in his new role. But his brother continued to handcuff him, as if he was afraid to unleash him.

He sank his fingers into the knot of his tie and yanked it loose. "You don't trust me."

"I wouldn't have given you the job if I didn't trust you."

"Then why the hand-holding?"

His brother's gaze darkened. "You've been knee-jerk in the extreme the last six months, Matty. You're like a cowboy with his guns drawn at all times."

"I'm hungry," Matteo growled. "Give me something to sink my teeth into and you will have my complete and utter focus."

"Exactly my thinking." Riccardo plucked a magazine from the surface of his immaculate desk and held it up. "Warren Davis just bought the Luxe Hotel chain."

Matteo nodded. The purchase by the world's third richest man, an investment genius revered around the world, had made headlines a few weeks back. The confirmation of a deal that had been in the works for months. "I looked into it a while ago," he told Riccardo. "Patreus has it locked up for another three years."

"Not any more they don't." Riccardo tossed the magazine on his desk. "Davis is reevaluating all suppliers."

He frowned. "How do you know that?"

"I played poker with a close friend of his on Monday night. De Campo is now in the running for marquee wine partner."

Matteo sucked in a breath. "That's a six- or seven-million-dollar contract, minimum."

"Ten." The hungry light he knew so well flared in his brother's eyes. Antonio De Campo, their father, had built De Campo into a global wine empire. Riccardo, with his endless thirst to make his mark, had driven it even higher with the restaurant division he was building. But for the core wine business, which was still all-important, this was huge. It would mean De Campo would be featured in every single one of Luxe's legendary restaurants worldwide. The coveted locations where politicians, princes and A-list celebs dined…

Merda. This was massive. "What next then?"

"Davis has put his daughter, Quinn, in charge of restaurant operations. She will be the final decision-maker on the wine contract. The Davises are doing a chemistry test with the four short-listed companies next week in Chicago. From there they'll pick the final two to pitch for the business."

"A chemistry test? What in God's name is that?"

"Warren Davis is all about the relationship aspect of business. Common ideals, common philosophies, he says, are the keys to creating a successful partnership. It's not always about what looks best on paper for him. The four short-listed companies are all great candidates. It will be the chemistry we have with Davis and his daughter that will put us in the final two."

Helpful then, that Matteo happened to be a master at persuading a female to do his bidding. "What form will this chemistry test take?"

"A cocktail party at the Davis residence."

Matteo's lip curled. "Like sharks circling one another..."

"Pretty much." Riccardo rhymed off two of the largest spirit companies in the world who had swallowed up smaller regional winemakers and a niche producer out of southern Australia.

"Silver Kangaroo?"

Riccardo nodded. "They've been winning some big awards lately."

"Yes, but *odd*. They are so niche." He gave his head a shake. "Any idea which way they're leaning?

"Quinn, apparently, has her eye on Silver Kangaroo. *We* are considered an outside shot."

Against the odds. Exhilaration tightened his body, sent his blood coursing through his veins. Just the way he liked it. When was the last time he'd felt that rush? That elemental surge of adrenaline he needed to feel alive? If Quinn Davis preferred a pure wine player they had a shot. Now all he had to do was work his magic.

"Do we have any intel on Quinn Davis?"

"Tough, smart, Harvard-educated." His brother handed him a folder. "It's all in here."

Matteo took it and lifted a shoulder. "She'll be all right, then."

Humor darkened his brother's gaze. Riccardo had gone to Harvard, Matteo to Oxford. It was a standing debate between them which was superior.

Matteo leafed through the folder. "Quinn manages some of his companies for him, doesn't she?"

"*Si*. Most recently Dairy Delight. Warren is hoping her experience in the food sector will help revive Luxe's restaurants. They've been on a slow decline for years."

"*Dairy Delight?* They sell ice cream and burgers. How's that going to help bring Michelin three-star restaurants back to life?"

Riccardo shot him a warning look. "Do not underestimate her, Matty. Apparently she's a chip off the old block."

Yes, but she was a female. He'd never met one he couldn't have. If he was on his game, she'd be in the palm of his hand before he'd finished his first cocktail. His mouth tightened. He intended to be more than on his game. *All over* his game was more like it. Which didn't mean he *would* underestimate her. Women were like sleeping bears. All soft and cuddly until you awakened their inner beast. Which was precisely why you didn't go *there*.

He closed the folder. "Who's going?"

"You are."

He did a double take. "With you and Gabe?"

"I need to be in San Francisco for the restaurant opening and Gabe is in way over his head with the harvest right now. I can't pull him away."

A surge of anticipation fired through him. *Finally* he was back in the game. The deal was his to win.

Riccardo kept his gaze steady on him. "This is the most important contract we've negotiated in the history of De Campo. We win this, we enter a different stratosphere. You need to bring it home, Matty."

"Done."

His brother's eyes flickered at the belligerently confident note in his voice. Mistrust. It was still there.

His shoulders shot to his ears, blood pumped so rapidly into his head he thought it would explode. *"Do not say it,"* he bit out. "Do *not* say it."

"What happened with Angelique Fontaine can't happen again, Matty."

The liquid fire burning in his head became an all-consuming force that blurred his vision. He swung away and sucked in a deep breath. Then another. Fisted his hands by his sides until they numbed into a lifeless mass. "How long," he demanded hoarsely, "are you going to crucify me with that?"

"Bring me Luxe," his brother said deliberately, "and we're even."

Matteo bowed his head. Flexed his frozen appendages until the blood streamed back into his fingers. When he looked up, he sought, *demanded* an honest answer from his brother. "Why me? You could make time for this, Riccardo."

His brother rested that deadly sharp gaze of his on Matteo. "Because you are the only one who can win this. Quinn Davis is a man-hater. She will detest me on sight. Gabe could do it, but you are better. Not only do you have the charm but when you're on, Matty, you light up a room. You are electric."

He exhaled the breath lodged deep inside his chest. "Luxe is ours. I promise you that."

Riccardo nodded. "Absorb what Paige has put together and let me know if you have any questions."

Matteo tucked the file under his arm and headed for the door. His brain was already formulating his approach when Riccardo's low drawl reached him. "Matty?" He turned around. "I meant what I said. You are not, under any circumstances, to sleep with Quinn Davis."

All creativity fled. A muscle jumped in his jaw, his teeth clenching down so tight he thought they might shatter. "I heard you the first time. It can't happen. It won't happen. And I'm getting a little pissed you'd think I'd even go there."

Riccardo shrugged. "You're a complete wild card lately, Matty. They could announce the next shuttle expedition to the moon and I wouldn't be surprised to see your name on the list."

His insides tightened. "You *know* what I was going through. Why that happened with Angelique…"

His brother's gaze hardened into impenetrable steel. "It was a seven-million-dollar deal, Matty."

And he had brought it down like a house of cards.

He gritted his teeth. "I will win this deal for De Campo. That's all you need to be sure about."

His brother nodded.

Matteo stalked to the door. Sure he was going to charm Quinn Davis. Riccardo wanted to win. How did he *think* he was going to win? But sleep with her? Did his brother really think he wanted another two years in purgatory?

Damn. He needed a cold beer.

His mood hadn't improved by the time he was home at his new Meatpacking District loft, a bottle of said cold beer in his hand on the patio. Kicking back in a lounge chair, he devoured the file Riccardo's PA had compiled. Paige had been her usual ridiculously thorough self. It contained everything he ever needed to know about the Davis family and more. And photos. It did not escape him why his brother had warned him off Quinn Davis. She wasn't just beautiful, she was knock-your-socks-off stunning.

The photo Paige had included, taken at a charity event, hit him right where it would any libido-endowed male. Petite, curvy in a lush "take me to bed" kind of way, she had silky, thick, long dark brown hair and the most haunting green eyes he'd ever seen.

Gorgeous. And, apparently, a man-hater. His mouth curved. He could work with that.

He took a swig of his beer. Paige's notes were a gold mine of cocktail party intelligence. Quinn Davis had worked at Warren Davis's investment firm since graduating from Harvard and had earned progressively more responsibility at a pace that would have made most people's heads spin. It was clear from the opinion pieces that although many would have liked to think nepotism had played a role in her success, she had done it on her own. One business columnist commented she had an "eerily sharp brain like her father." Another that she was an "instant study." But the description that captured his attention was the one that branded her a "gladiator in the boardroom."

This was getting more interesting by the minute.

He flicked to a profile piece on her personal life. Or lack thereof. She either didn't have one or she was the most ultraprivate person he'd ever encountered. Twenty-seven years old, resided in Chicago, divorced from Boston blue blood lawyer, Julian Edwards, after one year of marriage. *One year?* He lifted a brow. What in God's name had happened there? And a graduate-level Krav Maga? The instructors he knew had attained that level but none of his buddies had gotten past an orange belt despite years of practice.

Interesting was not the word. Fascinating was more like it. His mouth quirked. No wonder her marriage had fallen apart. Quinn Davis had probably emasculated her husband within the first three months of marriage.

He scoured the file from top to bottom, then threw it on the concrete beside him. Resting his beer on his thigh he looked up at the lone star in the Manhattan sky that never seemed to get truly black. An image of all three De Campo brothers—Riccardo, Gabriele, Matteo—walking into the boardroom of the second largest airline in Europe flashed through his head. That day in Paris had been their chance to make their mark on a company ruled for forty years by their despotic father, Antonio. It was Riccardo's first high-profile deal as CEO. They had been pumped, sky-high with adrenaline, the seven-million-dollar deal to supply the airline with its house wines firmly within their grasp.

They'd nailed the presentation. Had gone out to cele-
brate that night at a local bar. But after the adrenaline had
worn off, Matteo's recent all-encompassing grief over the
loss of his best friend, Giancarlo, had stormed back. Nothing had been enough to contain it—to make the guilt and
pain go away. The effort to keep up a happy face with his
brothers had been excruciating, ending with him seek-
ing solace in the arms of a beautiful woman. Except that
woman had been the daughter of Georges Fontaine, the
CEO of the airline. She worked for Fontaine, had been
on the executive team they'd pitched to. She'd also been
throwing herself at Matteo the entire time they'd been in
that boardroom.

He had reasoned Angelique Fontaine was a grown
woman capable of making her own decisions. But when
he'd made it clear the next morning he wasn't interested
in anything long-term, Angelique had gone straight to her
father. And De Campo's chance to put its wine on over half
a million flights a year had gone with her.

Angelique had branded him a callous son of a bitch.
Georges Fontaine had been furious. It had been the
worst mistake in judgment in Matteo's thirty-two-year-
old life.

He shifted on the chair, the memory of his brothers'
faces when Georges Fontaine had called the deal off physically painful to remember. Burned so indelibly into his
mind it was like a mental scar that never healed. Shock.
Disbelief. Disappointment.

The disappointment had been the worst.

He set his beer down on the concrete with a jerky movement. He had been in pain. But Riccardo was right. It
shouldn't have mattered.

Resting his head against the back of the chair, that lone
star blinking at him like a beacon—like his path to re-
demption—he knew this was his chance to finally put his

demons to rest. To move on. He would win this deal if it was with the last breath he had. Despite the odds that were stacked against him.

Unfortunately, the stakes had never been higher.

CHAPTER TWO

WARREN DAVIS'S REDBRICK Georgian Revival home in the Hyde Park neighborhood of Chicago shone with a century-old elegance in the early evening light. It had been an unusually steamy summer day, climbing into the hundreds, the haze that had blanketed the city just starting to lift. Cooler night air whispered across the tops of the tall pine trees that stood like sentinels on either side of the mansion, wafting through the window of Quinn Davis's room as she watched the heads of some of the world's biggest spirit companies arrive for the cocktail meet and greet.

The air might be cooler now, but the focused, intent look on each megapowerful man's face as he arrived promised a heated competition. Winning was all that mattered to men of this caliber. She'd lived with one her whole life—the most alpha of them all in Warren. And she couldn't deny, she was their female equivalent. Except she had to be even tougher, stronger and more focused than all of them to survive. A female warrior in a male-dominated world.

She was fascinated to see how the men would play. How the testosterone party would unfold.

Every single one of them, as they arrived in everything from custom-made suits to cowboy hats, looked up at the American flag billowing from the porch, and undoubtedly, reminded himself again of its significance. Warren Davis was a national symbol of what made America great—a billionaire philanthropist who gave away more of his money than he kept. A patriot and financial genius who advised presidents on monetary policy and led social commentary. He was the man everyone wanted to know. The man people paid three and a half million to have lunch with at his charity auction date for the homeless, in the hopes they might pick up a miniscule amount of his brilliance.

He was also, as a stroke of fate would have it, the man who had chosen, along with his Irish wife, Sile, to adopt Quinn as a baby when her young Southern parents had been unable to care for her. Warren and Sile had barely brought their new baby home when Sile had miraculously fallen pregnant after years of unsuccessful fertility treatments and given Quinn her sister and best friend, Thea.

Thea, even now still primping herself in front of the mirror, fussing over yet another choice of hairstyle. Quinn grimaced and levered herself away from the window. "Please pick one and be done."

Her sister squinted at herself and gave a dramatic sigh. "How am I supposed to choose with four of the world's most powerful men coming for cocktails? This has to be daddy's *best idea ever*. I mean, he has two single daughters right?"

Since her marriage to Julian had been a certified disaster, yes, that did put her squarely in that category. Not that she had any plans to ever repeat her mistake.

"Tonight is about getting to know potential partners," she told her veterinarian sister, who knew as much about business as she knew about changing a tire. "Not speed dating."

"Ha." Thea shot her a rebellious look. "With a cattle and wine baron in the house, not to mention delicious Matteo De Campo.... You think I'm missing out on *that* opportunity?"

Quinn smiled. She wished, sometimes, she had just a

little bit more of her younger sister's boundless enthusiasm for life. For love. But she wasn't sure she'd ever even had it to start with.

"Daniel Williams is beautiful," Quinn drawled. "I'll give you that."

Thea tossed her long blond hair over her shoulder. "I fancy living on his ranch. I can take care of the animals while he tends to his vineyard. Although—" she put a finger to her mouth in a thoughtful gesture "—I'd gladly forget all about the animals if Matteo De Campo deemed me fit to give a second look. *He* is one real-life animal I wouldn't mind taming."

Quinn gave her a look from beneath perfectly manicured brows. "Matteo De Campo is a notorious playboy who couldn't take a woman seriously if she were the only one left on the planet. And even then," she declared, her lip curling, "he'd find it difficult to get past his love affair with himself."

Thea threw out her hands. "Who *cares?* I hear a woman can't be in the same room as him without throwing her panties at him. He's *that* hot."

"He's not *that* good-looking." Unless you went for the smoldering male à la perfume commercials who looked like he'd keep you up all night.

Her sister caught the gleam in her eye. "See? Undeniable. You need to throw off that 'I was married and it sucked' baggage and move on. Live a little."

Quinn's heart clamped into the hard little ball that seemed to be its permanent state since Julian had left. No one but her knew the truth of her marriage. The public line had been irreconcilable differences. What happened behind Davis doors was never revealed.

Better the truth of her marriage not be.

She forced a wry smile to her lips. "Don't go throwing

your panties at Matteo De Campo. Not only will he break your heart, but he'll be mad when he loses the bid."

Thea drew her brows together. "Have you already decided then?"

"No, but De Campo's probably last on the list." She wanted Danny William's Silver Kangaroo. The small, award-winning Australian winery was the perfect eclectic fit for what she wanted to do with the Luxe brand.

"Daddy likes De Campo," Thea said, following her to the door. "He said their new Napa wines are brilliant."

"*Daddy* isn't making the decision."

Thea gave her a sideways look. "When are you going to stop trying to live up to this vision of perfection he expects? You could do that every day for the rest of your life and it'd still never be enough."

Possibly true. But she was a little afraid she'd die trying. This was the biggest opportunity of her career and she intended to make her mark with it.

She did have to maintain *some* objectivity, she told herself as she and Thea made their way down the winding staircase, through the massive drawing room and out the French doors that led to the gardens where the cocktails were being served. It was only fair after all, even if she knew the choice she was going to make in the end.

The terrace in the middle of the immaculately landscaped gardens was buzzing as they arrived, the two CEOs of the larger spirit companies with their wives in attendance, while Daniel Williams and Matteo De Campo had obviously elected to fly solo, to Thea's delight.

Surprising. Matteo's Hollywood ex had been moaning in the tabloids about all of her ex-lover's women, but not one was in sight tonight.

All eyes settled on her and her sister. Blonde Thea glowed with the prospect of meeting her Prince Charming while her dark-haired alter ego felt herself the instant target of four sets of male eyes. Not because she was beautiful, although she knew that she was. But because she was their ticket to massive international sales growth.

They were sizing her up. Waiting to see if she was as impressive as her track record. It sat on her shoulders with the almost oppressive weight that being Warren Davis's daughter always had. She not only had to be better than the rest, she had to be ten times better.

It was exhausting.

Thea sucked in a breath. "I really may have to forgo my ranch-living plans. *He* is just unreal."

Quinn didn't have to ask which man her sister was talking about, because Matteo De Campo's laserlike gaze was focused on her and it was like being in the path of an undeniable force of magnetism the likes of which she'd never experienced before. She'd met a lot of good-looking men. Her husband had been stunning…but he—*he* was something else. Unblinking, unashamedly approving of what he saw, his gaze took every inch of her in, right down to her toes. She swallowed hard. Shifted her weight so both designer-covered feet absorbed the impact.

"I hear he has a tattoo," Thea whispered. "Hot, right?"

Quinn couldn't help but wonder where on that tall, lean, muscular body it was. The dark suit that covered him was exquisite. The body better.

She found herself gaining a bit more respect for his legions of cast-offs as she returned his deliberate inspection. A woman might risk losing some self-respect over *that*. The photographs she'd seen of the youngest De Campo had been all about his lust for life, his freewheeling persona— the thick, unruly dark hair, the devil-may-care smile. But tonight, the hair was cropped close to his head so the sexy dark stubble that covered his square jaw showcased the perfection of his face. His expression was not the relaxed, indolent picture the tabloids loved to print. It was as intent as the night. Deliberate. Focused.

Damn. The "I am a sexy beast" stubble really worked for him.

She met his gaze, the amused half smile that curved his lips making her back stiffen. He was waiting for her to fall flat on her face. Waiting for her to fall all over him like every other woman did. She lifted her chin. He was so, so wrong on that. Julian had taught her well. The last thing any woman should trust was a pretty face in an expensive suit.

Summoning the cool, untouchable look she did so perfectly, she walked to her father's side. He made the introductions, the two spirit company CEOs first, then the two younger men. All four were impressive, charismatic personalities who would stand out in a crowd from the pure power they exuded like a second skin. But even Daniel Williams, the golden-haired wine-and-cattle baron who looked like he'd just walked out of a cigarette commercial seemed to fade into the background with Matteo De Campo standing beside him. Silver-gray, she registered as she shook his hand. Matteo's eyes were the exact color of the Chicago sky before a summer storm caused all hell to break loose.

Fitting then to feel that shiver slide up her spine.

"Quinn," he murmured, keeping his gaze locked on hers as he folded his big, warm hand around her fingers. "A stunning name for a stunning woman."

Her stomach did a funny roll as she retrieved her hand, the imprint of his fingers burning into hers. *Is he for real?*

"It's a pleasure to meet you, Mr. De Campo," she murmured smoothly. "Although I feel as if I should already know you with all the tabloid attention you've been getting lately."

He blinked, that one quick movement her only indication the gibe had landed. "Matteo, *per favore*," he invited in a smooth, whiskey-soaked tone she was sure played a large part in how he slayed women. "And surely, Ms. Davis, you know better than to believe everything you read in the tabloids."

"Where there's smoke there's usually fire, Mr. De Campo."

A wry smile curved his lips. *"A volte."*

She lifted a brow. "I'm sorry, I don't speak Italian."

"Sometimes," he drawled. "Sometimes there is, Ms. Davis."

Her father flashed her a sharp look. Her head snapped back just like it had when she was ten and being rebuked at the dinner table for talking too much when the adults were conversing. Her shoulders came up and she summoned the exquisite manners the Davis family was legendary for. "Lovely to have you with us tonight."

Matteo's eyes glimmered as he held up the bottle he was carrying. "My brother Gabriele wanted you to have this. It's the first bottle off the line of this year's Malbec."

The vintage that had the whole North American wine industry talking about it. The first bottle of the year at that. How very smooth. "I'm honored," she murmured, wrapping her fingers around the bottle. "It's a brilliant wine. Thank you."

Score one for Matteo De Campo.

"And this," he added, pulling two small silver-wrapped packages out of his jacket, "is a little taste of Tuscany for you both."

He handed the tiny packages to her and Thea. Thea nearly fell over herself thanking him. Quinn thought it was a little over the top, but the look on the other men's faces pronounced it an act of genius.

Two–nil.

Too bad she wasn't a fan of doing the predictable thing.

She took the gifts inside, then spent the evening soaking up the time with each prospective partner, doing as much reconnaissance as she could before she made her short list of two. Nothing surprised her about her conversations. In fact, she grew even more certain that Silver Kangaroo was the right choice. De Campo, in her mind, was too smug, too established a brand to fit with Luxe's new direction. But she owed Matteo her time. He was the only one she hadn't spoken to in depth, and although she'd like to tell herself she'd been too busy, she had the strange feeling she'd avoided him because he was a danger zone for her.

He was chatting with her father now, the two of them engulfed in a spirited debate about business issues. Her stern father had clearly fallen under the spell of Matteo's legendary De Campo charm. Bizarre, really, when Warren usually saw right through people.

She skirted around them and headed for the house to use the ladies' room. Her face ached from the polite smile she'd pasted on while the competitors plied her with information and assessed her comment by comment to find her hot spots, her weak spots. To see if she actually had a brain. Her feet burned in the stilettos that were her armor, as if a sharp heel could puncture the hurt she felt every time someone insinuated she'd gotten where she was because she was Warren's daughter. Her head throbbed from a fourteen-hour work day.

Sometimes being Quinn Davis was just much too much.

She sliced a wry glance at Thea flirting with Daniel Williams on the porch. She'd do her due diligence with Matteo when she came back. Then she was calling it a night. Dirty look from Warren or not.

Matteo felt his blood boil as Quinn Davis walked by him *yet again*. From her frosty reception of the presents he'd racked his brain to come up with, to her complete avoidance of his attempts to snare her time, she had been sending a loud and clear message. Either she didn't like him personally or De Campo didn't stand a chance. Neither was desirable, but he'd prefer it was a personal thing. That he could work with. A dislike of De Campo, not so much.

He stared after her, distracted by the sway of her delectable hips in the conservative summer dress that still managed to look sexy on her with that hourglass figure, despite the fact she had about as much personality as a block of ice. His fingers tightened around his glass. *Chemistry test.* What chemistry test? This was a farce.

Warren excused himself with a frown and went after Quinn. He watched them exchange words, Quinn's mouth tighten and her head incline. Then she continued on into the house. He clenched his teeth. What had he done to deserve this? That first moment they'd laid eyes on each other had been an intense, acknowledged male-female appreciation of each other's assets. Unmistakable. Man-hater Quinn might not like it, but she was attracted to him. That much he was sure of. And maybe *that* was the problem. A woman like her hated to reveal any chink in her armor.

She was going to be an even tougher nut to crack than he'd anticipated.

Good then that he'd had enough, *way more* than enough.

Daniel Williams ambled over and gave him a sympathetic look. "Still waiting? She's a piece of work, isn't she?"

He would normally have agreed but he knew enough to keep his mouth shut around the competition. He inclined his head toward Warren, instead. "That hour-long chat would have cost me three and a half million in auction. I'm not complaining."

The Australian's mouth quirked. "Touché. But Warren isn't making the decision, Quinn is."

Yes, she is. Matteo crossed his arms over his chest, antagonism heating him like a thirty-year-old scotch. "I heard

Quinn say she's been out to visit you guys. How long have you been working this?"

"Since they started negotiating for Luxe. About six months now. And she hasn't dropped the ice-queen act yet." Williams flashed a conspiratorial grin. "No surprise she's running an ice-cream company, eh?"

Matteo felt his insides combust. *Six months?* He'd been pursuing Quinn Davis's contract for *six months?* What chance did De Campo have? *Bloody chemistry test.*

He kept his temper in check. Just. "Seems like you're doing something right."

Williams leaned in, his voice dropping. "I've got that filly tied up tighter than tight, De Campo. Hate to say it 'cause I like you guys and we wine folk have to stick together. But this is pretty much a lock for us. Hate to see you waste your time."

He stiffened. "Wasting my time," he said quietly, pinning his gaze on the Australian's rough-hewn face, "would be competing in a game I can't win, Williams. And I don't see that happening."

His competitor's grin faded. "Best of luck, De Campo. I gotta tell you, you're a long, long shot. Hope you know that."

Matteo showed his teeth. "Just the way I like it."

Quinn came out of the house. "Would you excuse me?" he murmured. "My number is up."

Anger pressed ruthlessly down on him, burning brighter with every step he took toward the infuriating Quinn Davis. He could tolerate a lot of things, but people wasting his time was not one of them. Unfortunately this situation required him to be civil so he pasted a smile on his face and stopped in front of her. "Might I claim my time, do you think?"

Her long dark lashes came down to shield her expression. "Of course. I was just coming to find you. Warren said you wanted to see the koi pond."

He wanted to *dunk* her in the koi pond. He nodded instead and spread his hands out in front of him. "Please."

Quinn pressed her lips together as if this was the last thing she felt like doing and led the way. Her politely worded, disinterested questions as they made their way down the path into the rear of the gardens sent his temper to a whole new level. He pushed out his practiced spiel about De Campo's history, how the Tuscan and Napa vineyards were flourishing and why he thought their one-hundred-year-old company was the best choice for Luxe. It sounded flat even to his own ears because she so clearly didn't care. By the time they got to the koi pond, a beautiful little oasis that seemed to appear out of nowhere, he had blown a fuse.

She needed to throw him a scrap.

Quinn started spouting interesting nuggets about the pond. By the time she started telling him how they removed the tropical fish in the summer and took them inside, he'd had enough.

"I get the feeling you don't like me very much, Ms. Davis."

She blinked, then fixed him with that cool stare of hers. "It's not you I dislike, Mr. De Campo. It's your type."

The tabloid comment. Cristo, those stories. He shoved his hands in his pockets and narrowed his gaze on her lush, beautiful face. "Maybe you can elaborate on what my type is because I'm not sure I know."

"The global playboy," she supplied dryly. "The man who thinks he can manipulate everyone with his charm."

His gaze clashed with hers. "Funny thing is, I don't actually think that."

"'A stunning name for a stunning woman'? Come on, Mr. De Campo. Do you really talk like that?"

His lips stretched in a thin smile. "That wasn't a line, Ms. Davis. That was the truth."

Her small, even white teeth sank into a full bottom lip more suited to a woman who was actually a flesh-and-blood human being than an icicle. Too bad all of those just right, "take me to bed" curves were even more deadly in person. As in "take me to bed *right now.*" Because Quinn Davis was the epitome of a five-letter word he didn't normally care to use.

The smile faded from his lips. "Just how *much* of an underdog is De Campo?"

"Who said you were an underdog?"

"My position on your priority list," he said roughly. "If I were to rank it, I'd say Silver Kangaroo is your first choice, followed by H Brands and Michael Collins."

The flush that darkened her cheeks told him he was dead-on. He sliced his hand upward to push his hair out of his face, remembered he'd had it all chopped off and dropped it to his side. "Why are we even here if you aren't going to give us a chance?"

"You do have a chance." Her eyes flashed a taunting emerald. "Tell me why I should choose you, Mr. De Campo. I'm all ears. *Wow me.*"

He could think of a multitude of ways to *wow* this one, most of which could never be done in a boardroom...starting with shutting up that smart mouth of hers.

He bit his tongue and used reason instead. "You're big on Silver Kangaroo. I get that they're a hot brand, winning awards, but so are we. In fact, De Campo is doing things no one else is, as you know, with the Malbecs and Syrahs in Napa. Warren is big on made in the U.S.A. There's your angle."

She lifted a delicate shoulder. "I'm more interested in choosing the *right* brand. Made in the U.S.A. is nice to have."

"Good," he agreed. "Then I'm sure you know you'll get more personal attention from us than the big brands. How much love and devotion will Michael Collins or H Brands give you?"

"A lot, they've promised."

He lifted a brow. "You can see through a lie, can't you, Ms. Davis? Ultimately, the reason you *should* choose us comes down to a partnership. We're in the restaurant business. Our restaurants are hugely profitable. We can help you. *Guide* you."

Her gaze glittered. "I *run* a national chain of restaurants. I'm sure you couldn't have missed that fact."

"Fast-food restaurants," he qualified. "It's a very different industry."

The warning in her eyes intensified. "Not so different, Mr. De Campo. But you make a good point. You're a competitor. Why should we fatten your pocketbook, open sesame on our trade secrets so you can kill us later?"

He shook his head. "De Campo isn't interested in luxury dining. Our restaurants service the trendy, hip crowd. It would be synergy, not competition."

"What's to say you won't expand? You've opened five restaurants this year."

"It's not in our plans. We know where our niche is. Allow us to partner with you, share what we've learned."

Her gaze hardened to a chilly, wintry green. "I don't want your advice, Mr. De Campo. I want your wine."

Damn, but she was a pain in the butt. "Riccardo and I had dinner in your Park Avenue restaurant this week. We wrote down a list of ten crucial mistakes you're making that would put you back in the black. You may want to hear them given our restaurants have a profit margin unheard of in the industry."

Her gaze flickered. *Bingo.* She crossed her arms over her chest. "Go on."

"Put us through to the next round and I will."

Her brows tilted. "What if you don't make it? You have an opportunity now to make your case."

"I'll take my chances."

"Ah. A gambler too."

"Always. Tell me something, Quinn. You don't like being underestimated, do you?"

"Not particularly, no."

"Thought so. Funny then that Daniel Williams thinks he has you tied up tighter than tight."

"Excuse me?"

"I think his exact words were 'I've got that filly tied up tighter than tight, De Campo.'"

"Filly?" The full force of that green gaze sank into him. "He said that?"

"Just now, in fact. Ask him. And while you're at it, you might want to find out where he's staying. I could have sworn I saw him walk out of the hotel across from yours tonight. The one with the three-word name that is not the Luxe brand."

Quinn's mouth dropped open. She stood there gaping at him, then apparently realized what she was doing and slammed it shut. Matteo flashed her a grim smile. "Appearances are deceiving, aren't they? You think I'm a playboy? You think I manipulate with my charm? Sure I do. I appreciate women. I appreciated you the moment I saw you and I know the feeling was mutual." He lifted his shoulders in a careless shrug. "But the thing is, you aren't my type, Quinn. I prefer the warm, affable ones over the ice queens. So perhaps you can tuck away your claws and play fair. Judge De Campo on our track record, not your misguided presumptions of who you think I am. Or this chemistry test is going to be a joke."

He walked after that, afraid if he said anything else he would sink De Campo's chances.

If he hadn't already.

Quinn followed him back to the others. Gut churning, he grabbed a drink from the tray of a passing waiter. What in God's name was wrong with him? Hot-headed was not an emotion he would normally have associated with himself. Reckless at times, yes. But that woman was *impossible*. And his career depended on her.

He watched her interact with the others, visibly cool with Daniel Williams now. At least he'd made her think twice. If he'd guessed right, the Silver Kangaroo CEO's arrogant words would make a woman like her crazy. And maybe it would make her do exactly the *opposite* of what she'd been planning. Backed up by the sound reasoning he'd provided.

The thought he might have once again destroyed the biggest opportunity in De Campo's history kept him awake for much of the night as the monogrammed Luxe Hotel sheets stared him in the face. Eventually he threw them aside with a curse and got out of bed for a 5:00 a.m. run before his flight.

It would be a couple of days before he learned the fallout of his actions. Quinn had said they'd be informed the beginning of next week.

The only thing he knew for sure right now, he thought, grimacing and picking up his pace into a flat-out run through the park, was that he, the master of charm, had not only failed to ace the chemistry test, it had been an adjunct failure of epic proportions. Quinn Davis might actually hate him after last night.

CHAPTER THREE

MATTEO HAD JUST stepped into his loft after his flight back
to New York when his phone buzzed in his pocket. Riccardo no doubt, looking for the full debrief.

He dropped his bag on the entryway floor, pulled out
his phone and checked the caller ID.

Quinn.

His chest tightened like a vice. Fast. *Too fast?*

"Quinn."

"Congratulations, Mr. De Campo." Her tone was brisk,
businesslike. "De Campo has made Luxe's short list of
two."

He let out his breath in a long, slow exhale. Relief mixed
with the sweet taste of victory, a heady cocktail that made
his blood surge in his veins. "No doubt it was my sparkling
personality," he offered dryly.

"No doubt."

The wry undertone in her naturally husky voice made
him smile. He leaned back against the foyer wall and ran
his palm over the stubble covering his jaw. "I am thrilled,
of course, that you picked us. *Grazie.*"

"Thank my new head sommelier for swinging the vote.
One taste of Gabriele's Malbec and she was onside."

"Remind me to thank her."

"I think the better route would be to keep you well
away from her."

He lifted a brow. "Why would you say that?"

"She isn't as jaded about men as I am. I'd prefer not to have a train wreck on my team."

"I think you overestimate my allure, Ms. Davis."

"I think I don't. Thank you for the perfume, by the way. You didn't need to do that."

"I thought a little piece of Tuscany was apt. You like jasmine then?"

"I do."

"Good. It's one of the world's great scents."

"I assume this is one of your techniques? Plying women with expensive perfume?"

"One of the more rudimentary ones, yes," he admitted. "I also know my way around a kitchen. You'd be amazed how impressed women are by a man who can cook."

"I can only imagine." There was a pause. "I have no doubt about your…capabilities in any department you choose to apply yourself in, Mr. De Campo. Would next week suit to visit your Tuscan operations? I'd like to do that first, then show you two of our Caribbean properties we're reopening in St. Lucia so you can get a feel as to where Luxe is headed before we do the pitch in early August."

"Of course. Will cowboy Jack be along for the ride to the Caribbean?"

"If you're referring to Daniel Williams, then yes, he is the other half of the final two."

"Perfetto," he drawled, sarcasm lacing his tone. He was sure he could find a way for the Australian to stick his mouth in it again. It would be his pleasure. "We can do Tuscany whenever you like. Name the time."

"How about Friday? That way I don't miss the working week."

His lips twisted. God forbid the workaholic miss a day

churning out money for Davis Investments. "Shall I send the De Campo jet for you?"

"Thank you but I'm mandated by Davis rules to fly commercial. Demonstrates good corporate governance."

He shrugged. "The offer's there."

"Thank you."

"I do have one, nonnegotiable condition to us moving forward."

A pause. "Which is?"

"You need to start calling me Matteo."

He could have sworn he heard her smile. "I want your top-ten list, *Matteo*."

The Chagall he'd recently purchased at auction drew his eye, a vivid splash of color against the cream entryway wall. "Over a bottle of Brunello in Tuscany, Quinn. Bring a sweater for the *castello*. It gets chilly at night."

"Have you forgotten?" Her low, sardonic tone dripped across the phone line. "I'm already ice-cold."

Low laughter escaped him. "Why, Quinn Davis, I think you have a sense of humor."

"Don't go imagining things.… I'll have our admins connect on the details."

She disconnected the call. He slipped his phone back into his pocket and shook his head. As far as standoffish women went, it was his theory that some were cold and uninviting at their core, while others just pretended to be so for a whole variety of reasons. The latter category had always fascinated him. Often proved the biggest challenge *and* the sweetest reward. He'd bet his Chagall Quinn was one of them.

Too bad that particular challenge was off-limits. If his vow to swear off women wasn't enough of a reason to put Quinn in that category, his ten-million-dollar one was.

He settled in and called Riccardo, an intense feeling of exhilaration moving through him. They had made it to the pitch. That's all he needed. No one could beat him in a room. *No one.*

His cold beer on the patio that night tasted very sweet indeed.

I should have taken the De Campo jet. Quinn embarked her commercial flight in Florence stiff, sleep deprived and wanting to strangle the man who'd sat beside her on the London to Italy leg, humming incessantly in her ear. She could have used the luxury of Matteo's flying spa to actually get some work done considering she was too much of a control freak to sleep on planes. Instead, she'd done an excellent impersonation of a Quinn sandwich lodged between two overweight men on the seven-hour overseas flight, unable to move and completely unproductive. Then had come the humming.

She pulled up the handle on her carry-on and wheeled it through to the arrivals area of the tiny airport. Unproductive was the sore point here with the amount of work she had on her plate. Luxe was in far worse condition than she and Warren had ever imagined. When they'd started peeling back the layers and taken a hard look at the real financials—it was clear Luxe's former parent company had been hiding a multitude of sins, including the fact that the restaurant wing of the chain was bleeding money at light speed. The rosy glow of Luxe's heyday had long since passed and things were definitely on a downward spiral.

Enter Quinn Davis. Miracle worker.

She sighed and sat down on a bench to wait for her suitcase. She could do this. One step at a time, her mother had always told her when she was a little girl, fretting over some issue or another. Even at six, Quinn had been the girl waiting for the hammer to drop. Waiting for the pin to prick the bubble of her happy existence. The only girl in her first-grade class who had refused to get a dog because it might get run over by a car like her friend Sally's had.

As if, despite all of Warren's and Sile's efforts, she'd known at the core of her she was different. That her life wasn't destined to be the gilded storybook it had been presented as.

She closed her eyes against the pressure starting to build in her head. Hadn't she proven time and time again in her short career she could do the impossible? She just needed to get this whirlwind two-day trip to Italy over with and move on to solving her real headaches. Like the handful of her restaurants that were literally falling apart because they hadn't been renovated in so long. The local strikes that were paralyzing her Mediterranean locations. Completely incompetent management in others.

Luxe had seen better days. Her dream assignment was turning into a nightmare. Fast.

The baggage belt finally coughed to life and spit out her suitcase. Pulling up the handle she wheeled it and her carry-on through the barely there customs checkpoint and out into the Tuscan sunshine. The heat of the summer day burned down on her head and shoulders. She stopped, stripped off her cardigan and wrapped it around her waist, pushed her sunglasses to the top of her head and searched for a sign with her name on it. She found Matteo instead, leaning against an atrociously expensive-looking sports car. Dressed in an Oxford University T-shirt and jeans that molded his long legs into a work of art, he looked cool, elegant and very Italian. Also scorching, singe-yourself-on-him hot.

Quinn's hand flew to her head and the French twist she hadn't straightened since...when? London? She must look a sight. Her slacks were creased, her shirt had a coffee stain on it from where one of the men from her personal sandwich had dumped it on her and she was pretty sure she'd forgotten to wipe the breakfast cream cheese off her face. She reached up and swiped a palm across her mouth. What was it about the Italians that made you feel incredibly gauche just from your pure lack of style?

She had not expected her ride to be *him*.

He strolled toward her, his relaxed, indolent stride catching the eye of about twenty women around her. Her gaze dropped to the black lettering stretching across his biceps. *The tattoo*. Damn if it didn't give the whole package some serious edge.

Exactly what it didn't need. Her husband had been a pretty boy, the Ivy League son of a high-powered lawyer Warren had admired. Not Quinn's choice. His ego had required the kind of massive stroking it was impossible for one woman to administer. Unlike Matteo De Campo. He had it all built in. She doubted he'd had an uncertain day in his entire life.

The glitter in his gray eyes as he stopped in front of her said he hadn't missed her lustful look. She yanked in a breath of the fragrant, rose-scented Tuscan air. She needed to squash the physical attraction between them like a bug. Fast.

"You didn't need to come yourself," she murmured, caught off guard when he bent and pressed his lips first to one cheek, then the other. It was like being branded by a force she had no ability to cope with.

He drew back, his mocking glance sliding across her flushed face. "You're in Italy now, Quinn. We don't shake hands. We kiss."

She stepped back, wrapping her arms around herself. "You'll have to excuse my appearance. It's been a long day. I'm a mess."

"If that's a bad day," he murmured, his lazy gaze taking her in, "most women would kill to have more of them."

Her breath jammed in her throat. "You just can't help it, can you?"

"No," he agreed, smoky eyes laughing at her. "That's what playboys do, Quinn. Play. However," he drawled, picking up her bags and tossing them into the pitifully small backseat of the car, "I will endeavor to keep it to a bare minimum, just for you."

"You are too kind."

He held his hands up in a typically Italian gesture, then opened the passenger door for her. She slid in, absorbing the butter-soft interior of the car. "Fits the bad-boy image don't you think?"

The exotic car growled as he brought it roaring to life. She had to agree as he gunned it and they sped out of the airport that yes, it was sexy and so was the tattoo, which close-up, she could now see was in Latin, the beautifully scripted symbols set in a perfectly straight line across the hard muscles of his biceps. Unfortunately the Latin was mumbo jumbo to her. She was about to ask him what it meant when she clamped her jaw shut. Deciphering Matteo De Campo's tattoo was an activity better left for those actresses and models who were happy to let themselves fall for that type of meaningless charisma. She, on the other hand, knew better.

Matteo flicked her a sideways glance. "The *castello* is about an hour's drive. Feel free to relax and nap on the way. You look tired."

She grimaced. "I don't sleep on planes."

His mouth curved. "Don't tell me, you'd prefer to be flying it?"

"However did you know?"

"Just a wild guess. If you aren't going to sleep I'll pick your brain."

Pick her brain he did during the drive along the windy *autostrada* toward Siena. Commanding the powerful car along the highway's twists and turns with a fearless abandon that made her heart pound, he asked a series of excellent questions about Luxe's operations and mandate while at the same time managing to act as tour guide. His multitasking, expressive hand movements and excessive speed had Quinn grabbing for the door handle more than once.

"Any chance you can slow down?" she muttered after one particularly terrifying turn. "Or is that too much to ask of your playboy persona?"

His smile flashed white against his olive skin. "Too much. Driving in Italy is a blood sport. You'd be asking me to emasculate myself."

Not a chance, she thought grimly. It wasn't possible. Not with those mouthwateringly muscled thighs flexing beside her, drawing her attention every time he shifted gears. Or his big, beautifully tapered hands that looked as if they'd be masterful at any activity he pursued.... He was the type of ultradangerous male you wouldn't know you were in trouble with until you were way, *way* gone.

She lifted her gaze to the road, to the vibrant red poppies dotting a sea of green on its edge. That was enough of that.

Quinn focused on the information Matteo was imparting about Montalcino, the town where the *castello* was located. It had a bloodthirsty history, warred over for decades by its powerful foreign neighbors and even her own neighboring city-states back in the days before Italy had become a nation. The *castello* was actually a fortress, he relayed. It had played a strategic role in the struggles between the Sienese and the invading powers.

"The cellar is actually the old dungeon where the prisoners of war were held. It's quite a showpiece. We think it gives it great atmosphere."

That was one way of putting it. "They actually locked people up down there?"

"*Si.* Some of them died." He laughed at her horrified expression. "When my grandfather bought the *castello* and we renovated, we found two old skulls we keep on display."

She recoiled. "How very macabre."

He shrugged. "Wars happen. Have since the beginning of time."

They swept around a turn and a magnificent stone building came into view, perched on the top of a hillside, towering over the mountainous forests that surrounded it. Quinn gasped. "Is that it?"

He nodded. "The *Castello* De Campo. Dates back to the Middle Ages."

She took in the sprawling brawn of the imposing burnt-orange structure, its square turrets and tall watchtower like something out of a movie. "It's incredible."

Matteo pointed toward the terraced vineyards that extended from the top of the mountain to the bottom. "The De Campo estate is actually a constellation of vineyards. The different slopes and elevations of the mountain offer each varietal the optimum growing conditions. Some of the whites such as the Chardonnay, for instance, are planted further above sea level, where the nights are cool and the ripening season long, whereas the Brunellos, the king of our reds, thrive at a lower level."

"Margarite is obsessed with your Brunello."

"Who?"

"My head sommelier."

"So she should be," he murmured cockily. "We'll have one tonight."

She was so exhausted she might fall flat on her face if she drank anything. But Margarite would kill her if she passed up the opportunity to try the famous, lusty De Campo red.

"The scale is breathtaking," she said to him. "How many varietals do you produce?"

"Fifteen." He flicked her a glance. "Do you ride? I thought we would do the tour by horseback tomorrow."

"Not well," she admitted. She was suspicious of horses. They were big, heavy, unpredictable animals. Kind of like men. She didn't need either of them in her life.

It was impossible not to think how much more history De Campo had than Silver Kangaroo as Matteo parked the car in front of the magnificent *castello* and carried her bags inside. It was everywhere. In the century-old, mature vineyards surrounding the castle, in the family crest on the building as they came in, in the third generation of winemakers producing the glorious vintages here. Silver Kangaroo was only twenty years old. Although there was something to be said for such a young winery winning so many awards in such a short amount of time, it couldn't compare to De Campo in lineage.

Matteo led her into the magnificent tiled hallway of the west wing which was the personal residence of the De Campo family. With its cathedral ceiling and stunning frescos it was truly amazing. Like she'd walked into the home of royalty.

Matteo introduced her to Maria, the Italian housekeeper who had run the De Campo household since he was a boy, then led her up a winding staircase to a turret bedroom that took her breath away. The exposed brick walls of the *castello* extended into a double-arched stone wall that separated a sitting room with a fireplace from the bedroom and its huge canopied bed. The beautiful, rich fabrics covering the room cast everything in a golden, luxurious hue that might have been a royal princess's bedroom.

It evoked a strange feeling in Quinn. She'd spent much of her life feeling like the imposter princess. Her birth father, a factory worker in Mississippi, even now worked two jobs to make ends meet for his family. She knew because she'd hired a private detective to find them and learned the real truth about her adoption. Unlike the story she'd been fed by a well-meaning Warren and Sile, it hadn't been as simple as her mother having an affair with a married man and giving her up because of the complications of their relationship. Her mother had gone on to marry her father and they'd had another girl. Her sister.

To replace the girl they'd given away.

"Quinn?" Matteo was looking at her with a raised brow. "Everything okay?"

She blinked. "It's stunning, thank you. I can't imagine what it must have been like to grow up in a castle."

"I have stories." A wry smile tipped his mouth. "You can imagine the hiding spots three industrious boys found."

She smiled. "Some impossible to find ones, I'll bet. Will I get to meet your parents tonight?"

He shook his head. "Unfortunately, no. Antonio serves on the boards of a couple of major corporations. He's in London right now for meetings and my mother is in Florence where she prefers to stay."

Interesting arrangement. While her mother was alive, Warren would fly all night to get home to her. They hadn't spent a night apart that wasn't business. Her stomach twisted. In many ways, Sile's tragic death at a far-too-early age had turned her father into a different man. Taken the small amount of softness Warren possessed with her, his anger at her death so raw and all-consuming.

"Does seven suit for dinner?" Matteo asked. "If you sleep after that you should be able to get into the time."

"That's perfect, thank you."

"*Fino a stasera.* Until tonight…"

And why did even that sound sexy? She closed the door behind him and blamed it on the accent. Accents were always sexy on a man. His, particularly so.

She looked longingly at the bed. *Just a couple more hours,* she told herself, intending on showering first and catching up on email. But her eyelids burned from fatigue and she felt as if her body had been pummeled in a boxing match. Maybe a few minutes with her eyes closed on the high canopy bed in the beautiful, fairy-tale-ish room would refresh her enough to make it through dinner.

Help her figure out exactly how she was going to avoid the inescapable attraction she felt toward her host. Her reaction to him, she decided, curling up on the satin comforter, was probably due to the fact she hadn't looked at a man since Julian had left. Had buried herself in work lest the humiliation of it all become simply too much to bear. She hugged the pillow to her. Quinn never intended to feel that kind of humiliation ever again. From any man. So she was missing the gene that allowed her to be truly intimate with another person…. The way she'd survived in this world, the way she'd survived as a Davis was to shield her heart. To not let herself feel.

It was easier that way. To not *need* anyone. And she wasn't changing her strategy now.

Matteo knocked on the heavy wooden door of Quinn's suite just after seven, his game plan firmly in place. Ply her with an incomparable Brunello, impress her with the history and atmosphere of De Campo over dinner in the cellar and, most importantly, find out why she'd ranked them fourth on her list.

A piece of cake, as the Americans would say.

When there was no response to his knock, he rapped again, harder. Nothing. Strange. Quinn seemed like the overly punctual type. He was knocking on the two-inch-thick door a third time when it flew open and she stood before him, bleary-eyed, dark hair flowing over her shoulders in a jumbled mass of curls.

"I'm so sorry," she murmured. "I fell asleep."

He wasn't. She had the face of an angel when she wasn't

frowning. Her big green eyes had a sleepy, muted golden edge to them, an intense vulnerability he couldn't tear his gaze from. He had the feeling this was the *real* Quinn Davis. The softness behind the hard edge she liked to present to the world. Unfiltered.

His gaze drifted down over the flushed, rosy skin of her cheeks, her full, pouty lips that were the kind a man imagined wrapped around a certain part of his anatomy...

Matteo's body temperature soared. Quinn cleared her throat. The flicker of sexual awareness that replaced the vulnerability in her eyes slammed into him with the force of a hammer. *Merda.* Where had he ever gotten the impression this woman was cold? Or maybe it was just that she was a perfect combination of fire and ice?

Quinn dropped her gaze to somewhere around his shoulder and waved a hand at him. "Give me five minutes and I'll be ready."

He nodded. The click of the door brought back his sanity. Bringing Quinn Davis to her knees in that particular fashion might have been the natural order of things for him—but, regrettably, he needed to use his brain on this one, not his body.

Unfortunate. But not nearly as unfortunate as the consequences of not playing this one by the book.

Quinn emerged in a navy dress that made the most of her voluptuous curves in her usual, conservative fashion. Her ultracomposed, cool demeanor was firmly back in place.

"I hope this is okay?" She smoothed her hands over her hips. "You didn't specify."

"Perfetto." He nodded. "I'm sorry, I should have mentioned it was just the two of us dining in the cellar. Anything goes."

A wary look crossed her face. His lips curved. "I promise my best behavior, Quinn. We can recite every last statistic on De Campo over dinner. I'll even tell you what we polish the floors with."

"Ha, ha," she murmured, long lashes coming down to veil her expression. "I wasn't worried."

Si, *you were.* He wasn't the only one having a hard time handling the chemistry between them, but he instinctively knew Quinn Davis had to feel in control of a situation for him to accomplish anything tonight, so he let it go.

Fortunately, he was an expert at the slow, insidious penetration of a woman's defenses.

He took her on a tour of the west wing, showing her the centuries-old library, the opulent, chandelier-encrusted ballroom and the music room with the grand piano. When she had a suitably glazed-over look at the pure scale of things, he took her through the stone hallways to the east wing where the restaurant was just starting to fill up with locals and tourists. She was unfailingly polite and charming to his chef, making Guerino Pisani smile broadly and insist she come back after dinner to let him know how she liked it. Was it just him, the playboy, she disliked then?

His ego slightly dented, Matteo led Quinn down the dark, winding stone stairwell to the cellar. "You weren't kidding," she murmured, craning her neck to take in the two ancient skulls that sat backlit in one of the alcoves. "Do you know who they belonged to?"

"We assume someone unfit for a Christian burial. Spaniards, the French, the forces of the Holy Roman Emperor Charles V, they were all imprisoned down here. Also the Aldobrandeschi and the Guelphs of Florence—powerful families at war with the Sienese."

She followed him down the hallway to the cellar. The stone walls on either side of them were thick slabs of rock that would have made escape impossible. Collections of medieval weapons—swords, pikes, helmets and breastplates—were lit on either side of them.

"It all seems so brutal," Quinn said, giving them a long look.

"It was. It was hand-to-hand combat in its most savage form."

That feeling of brutality remained in the majestic cellar Matteo's grandfather Alfonso De Campo had built. The exposed brick walls rose thirty feet, tiny bar-encased windows the only natural light entering the room. The muted lighting hinted at a history of darkness. But it was the feeling that souls had suffered here that got into your bones. Even with all the elegant touches Alfonso had included—the dark walnut shelving that rose fifteen feet high to house De Campo's most precious vintages and the elegant, hand-turned showpiece of a bar.

"It's breathtaking," Quinn murmured, wide-eyed. "Did they *execute* prisoners down here?"

His mouth tilted. "From what I've been told, most died from existing injuries."

She didn't look so reassured by the response. He held a chair out for her at the candlelit table for two the serving staff had set in the middle of the room. Then he sat down opposite her and swept his hand toward the bottle of wine breathing in the middle of the table. "You'll have some?"

She scanned the label. The Brunello he'd chosen was the highest-ranking bottle in De Campo's one-hundred-year-old history. Apparently, its significance wasn't lost on Quinn, a wry smile curving her mouth. "Refuse the 1970 De Campo Brunello? I think not."

He poured the rich dark red, almost brown liquid into their glasses and held his own up. "To a successful partnership."

She tilted her glass in a mocking salute. "So confident."

"I don't intend to lose, Quinn."

"Then let the best candidate win." Her green gaze glittered as she lifted her glass and swirled its dark contents around the edge. She closed her eyes and breathed the wine in. He found himself hypnotized by the way she gave herself over to the full sensual experience. Quinn Davis was *definitely* scorching hot on the inside. The type who would be more than a match for any man. The question was, did she ever drop that rigid exterior and let herself go?

Stretch out like a cat and let a man pleasure her until she screamed?

She opened her eyes. Looked directly into his. He was not nearly quick enough to wipe the curiosity off his face. A rosy hue stole over her golden skin, her gaze dropping away from his.

He could work with this.

"So," she murmured huskily, after their food had been served, "give me your list."

He sat back in his chair and balanced the Brunello on his knee. "The wine list in your Park Avenue property is far too big. You're giving people too much choice. Distracting them. You need to allow your sommelier to do his job and sell the wines."

She frowned. "People like choice. I like choice. I hate it when I go to a place that tries to tell me what I want to drink."

"*Si,* but you have too much choice. The night Riccardo and I were there, a couple at the table beside us were all set to splurge on an expensive bottle, but by the time they got through your monstrosity of a list, they gave up and ordered a midend vintage they were familiar with. Your sommelier," he drawled, "never made it to their table that night."

"We're short-staffed there," she said defensively.

"It was a Tuesday night at six. There were empty tables."

She was silent. Pursed her lips. "Go on…"

"You need more beautiful women working the bar."

She lifted a brow. "So men can go ogle them and spend

their money? This is a high-end restaurant I'm running, Matteo, not a strip joint."

"Precisely. Seventy-five percent of the patrons at the bar that night were men—financial power players having a drink after work. Those types are all about the eye candy. You put a beautiful woman in front of them, they'll stay longer, drink more and I guarantee, they'll keep coming back."

"I suppose I should have them in short skirts, too?"

"Sex sells, Quinn."

She sighed and leaned back in her chair. "Sometimes I think life would be so much easier if I were a man. You are such simple creatures."

He smiled at that. "If you mean honest and straightforward about how we feel without a hundred pounds of analysis spread on top of it, then *si,* it's true."

"But in being that way, you miss many of the subtleties of life."

"Care to give an example?"

"I'd prefer you finish your list."

By the time he had and they'd eaten dinner, Quinn had the glaring feeling she'd vastly underestimated how valuable De Campo could be in helping her dig Luxe out of the mess it was in. Matteo was clearly a brilliant businessman and a marketing genius. De Campo *was* making scads of money at its übertrendy wine bar locations on the East and West Coasts. She'd done the research.

"You make some very good points," she conceded, pushing her empty plate away. "But there still remains the fact you are competition for us in the restaurant space."

He shook his head. "It's not the same clientele. Go sit in one of our wine bars. The customer is ten years younger at least. They do not have the disposable income to eat at Luxe."

Her gaze sharpened. "How would you guarantee you wouldn't compete with us in the future? Write it into the contract?"

He flinched, a slight, almost imperceptible movement. "We could talk about that."

She pressed her lips together. "It's a problem. I agree that there are synergies there. But I can't sell this to the board if we're going to be competing against each other."

"Who's to say Silver Kangaroo won't get into the restaurant business? You can't know what's going to happen in the future."

"But I can hedge my bets. Make my decisions based on the facts I have now."

He picked up the wine and poured the last of it into their glasses. It occurred to her she should probably refuse any more but the legendary Brunello was just too good to turn down.

He fixed that intense dark stare on her, the one that made her pulse jump all over the place. "Why fourth, Quinn? Why originally rank us fourth when you so clearly want a pure wine play, not a big behemoth."

Maybe the wine was loosening her tongue, but she decided he deserved to know. "In my mind, De Campo is an arrogant, self-satisfied brand. Yes, you make exceptional wine. Your lineage is impeccable. But you represent what Luxe *used* to be. Not where we're going. Silver Kangaroo is young, vibrant and fresh. A bit on the eclectic side. It fits perfectly with where I intend to take the Luxe brand."

A frown furrowed his brow. "De Campo is not an arrogant brand. A proud brand—yes. A brand with a century of heritage behind it—yes. But arrogant? You're wrong."

She tilted her head to one side. "I beg to differ."

"I have third-party brand studies that will *show* you you're wrong. That we appeal to a young, hip demographic."

"Brand studies are a self-serving exercise in making a

company feel good about itself," she countered. "It's an instinctual feeling I have, Matteo, and at the end of the day, that is how I will make my decision. Instinct."

Frustration glinted in his eyes. "You need to visit Gabriele in Napa. He is light-years ahead of Silver Kangaroo."

She nodded. "I will if time permits."

A server came to take their dishes away. "That was fantastic," she murmured, sure she could crawl into bed right now and sleep for twenty-four hours. "Maybe I should steal Guerino away from you."

He flashed a lazy smile. "Sorry. He'll never leave Italy."

"So sad." She tried to ignore how the dark stubble that covered his jaw was even more pronounced tonight as he spoke to the waiter in Italian. How it took his rakish good looks to a whole new dangerous level. But the warmth from the wine had turned her limbs into mush and her brain along with it. He had been mentally undressing her earlier, she was sure of it, and what had she done? Just let him keep on doing it. Insane, really, when this was all about business and this was Matteo they were talking about. The playboy who couldn't keep it in his pants.

Unfortunately that didn't stop her from studying his beautiful, elegant hands as he gestured to the server. It made her think of a quote she'd read in one of the tabloids while getting her hair done. One of Matteo's exes—the curator of a Manhattan art gallery—had made an incredibly blunt comment about how he'd been the best she'd ever had. Then had gone on to suggest she'd like to sample him again—all while dating the studlike quarterback of New York's pro football team.

He couldn't be that good. Could he? Or would those gorgeous hands be the perfect instrument to seduce a woman slowly, taking the time to savor her?

"Quinn?"

Her gaze flew guiltily to his. "Sorry?"

The grooves on either side of his mouth deepened. "Crème caramel or chocolate torte for dessert? Personally, I think Guerino's crème caramel is the best in Italy."

"Definitely the crème caramel." She might even manage to spoon some in her mouth before she did a faceplant in it.

Matteo relayed their choice to the server, then miraculously produced another bottle of Brunello. She held up a hand. "No more wine for me, thank you."

"I'll drink most of it," he said smoothly. "Live a little."

Her shoulders stiffened. Julian had said that to her all the time in that condescending, highbrow voice of his. *"Live a little, Quinn. Show me you can have some fun or you might drive me elsewhere."*

"Just half a glass," she said quietly.

"That was a joke, you know," he murmured, his gaze on her face. "Although you are known to be a workaholic. Just as driven as your father, insiders say."

Impossible. She'd never met a human being on this earth as driven as Warren. Her mouth twisted. "And what else did your intelligence turn up?"

"You made the top thirty under thirty business people in America this year. One of only two women. That must have made Warren proud."

Questionable. He hadn't much commented even though she'd been aching for him to. Quinn took a sip of the heady wine. Rolled it around her mouth and set the glass down. "No matter what people like to believe, there is still a glass ceiling for women. But I had advantages from the start."

"*Si*, but you've also had the disadvantage of being very beautiful. Many men don't take that seriously."

"Do you?"

His smile flashed white in the candlelight. "I've never underestimated a woman in my life, beautiful or otherwise. You would rule the world if men weren't physically stronger."

He looked genuine when he said that. Quinn had the ghastly idea she might actually like Matteo De Campo after these couple of days. Which was really, really not a good idea.

"So," she murmured, taking another sip of her wine, "what else was in your report?"

"The usual. Harvard, your rapid climb up the corporate ladder…" An amused glitter entered his eyes. "I have to say, the graduate-level Krav Maga caught me off guard. Interesting choice."

How had he found out about that? She never talked publicly about it. Went to the most discreet school in Chicago specifically to avoid that type of publicity.

She waved her hand at him, brushing it off. "It's an outlet."

"Hardly." That smoky, perceptive gaze stayed on hers. "Krav Maga is a street-fighting martial art, Quinn. The Israeli army trains its soldiers in it. It's hardly a casual outlet."

She shifted in her seat. And lied. "A girlfriend was doing it. It suits my competitive personality."

It would also make any man think twice about putting his hands on her ever again.

"Since we're trading interesting facts about one another," she said, changing the subject, "I'm intrigued by the tattoo. What does it mean?"

He touched his fingers to his biceps, as if he'd forgotten it was there. "It means 'never forget.'"

"Never forget what?" The words tumbled out of her mouth before she could stop them.

Matteo's gaze darkened to the deep slate of gunmetal. "My best friend, Giancarlo, died in a car accident recently. It was pointless. Unnecessary."

Oh. The way he said *unnecessary* sent a chill through her. The grief she saw in his eyes was something she knew all too well. *Dammit,* she castigated herself, she should not have asked that. The wine had been a bad, bad idea.

"I am so sorry," she murmured huskily, needing to say something into the heavy silence. "I lost my mother when I was ten. It makes you question everything, doesn't it?"

He nodded. "*Si.* It does."

The conversation stumbled after that. There was a darkness surrounding Matteo that contrasted strikingly with his earlier charming demeanor. When they'd finished dessert, he suggested she must be tired. She nodded and said that she was. Her head was starting to spin now. It was way past time for her jet-lagged body to be in bed.

They stopped by the kitchen where she gave Guerino her compliments, then walked over to the west wing. On the circular, steep stairwell to her turret bedroom, her head started to spin in a dizzying pattern that made the ascent in four-inch heels particularly challenging. Halfway up, her shoe caught in a rivet. She stumbled and teetered in the ridiculously high designer heels, and would have fallen if Matteo hadn't been behind her. He cursed, swept his arm under her knees and caught her up in his arms.

"Wh-what are you doing?" She dug her fingers into his muscular shoulders and held on for dear life.

"Making sure you don't break your neck," he muttered, carrying her up the last flight and down the hallway to her room. "Why you women wear those heels is beyond me."

She was too busy registering that wow, he was strong and so hot carrying her like this to pay much attention to the rebuke. He smelled delicious, too, the spicy, exotic scent of his aftershave filling her nostrils.

"I think I might have overdone the wine," she offered faintly as he set her down on the floor outside her room. He kept his hands around her waist as if scared she would keel over, his fingers burning into her skin like a brand. Quinn looked up at his gorgeous, sexy face, at the dark stubble she was dying to run her fingers over and told herself this was business.

Business. Business. Business.

The heat that arced between them like a living, breathing thing was not. It had been there from the moment she'd laid eyes on him and it was getting worse. The reluctant but oh-so-interested glitter in those smoky gray eyes wasn't helping.

"Ice-cold?" he drawled. "I think not, Quinn."

The heat pooling in her abdomen rose up to her face. For the first time since Julian had walked out on her two years ago, *she* was interested. She wanted, badly, to kiss a member of the opposite sex. And not just any member of the opposite sex. Matteo De Campo!

CHAPTER FOUR

IF IT HAD BEEN any woman other than Quinn Davis that Matteo had his hands on, if he hadn't just plied her with a bottle of Brunello and perhaps most importantly, if he hadn't promised his brother he'd keep his hands off her, Matteo would have stepped in, closed his hands firmer around her tiny waist and taken what she was so obviously offering.

Her forest-green eyes were hazy with desire and a curiosity that hit him square in the solar plexus. Her hips were soft under the span of his hands, her body primed for an exploration he was oh so ready to give her. And that perfume she was wearing, the one he'd given her, *merda,* did the spicy scent do something to him.

However, this *was* Quinn Davis standing in front of him, a tipsy Quinn Davis, and his fantasies had to stop here. He switched off the part of his brain that said to hell with it, lifted his hands from her with an exaggerated movement and stepped back. "See, Quinn?" A taunting smile curved his lips. "I can keep my hands to myself."

She planted a hand against the wall to steady herself, a defiant glitter stirring to life in her eyes. "Too much wine and a brief moment of madness. Don't flatter yourself thinking it would have gone anywhere."

He quirked a brow. "You don't think so? I may be all

kinds of arrogant, Quinn, but I know when a woman wants me to kiss her."

Her lush mouth parted, then slammed shut. At a loss for words. It might just have been the best part of the whole evening.

"Breakfast at eight tomorrow." He waved his hand in the direction of the family dining room. "We'll take it downstairs. And wear something appropriate for horseback."

She sunk her teeth into her bottom lip. "I told you I don't ride well."

"Not to worry, I have a gorgeous, even-tempered mare for you to ride. You'll love her."

She didn't look convinced.

"Good night," he murmured. "I'm at the end of the hall if you need anything."

The look she flashed him said it would be a cold day in hell before she ventured into his bedroom. Laughing inwardly, he turned on his heel and left.

If she only knew the things he could do to her.

With his brain on New York time and unable to sleep, Matteo headed down to the study, called Riccardo and told him to get working on a solution for Quinn's competitive concerns. "The board will never approve a clause in the contract," his brother dismissed. "We'll have to find another way."

"That's why they pay you the big bucks," Matteo inserted. "Find it."

His brother's husky laughter echoed in his ears. He put the phone down, pushed to his feet and paced to the window. The lights from the *castello* cast an amber glow over the surrounding hills, their peaks looming dark and endless the farther the eye traveled. The view was usually enough to bring him peace, but tonight he knew how steep his journey was about to get. He needed to convince Quinn that all this was what she should sign De Campo for. That no vineyard anywhere in the world produced vintages as fine as theirs or was as impressive. Which was what tomorrow's tour would do.

What concerned him more was Quinn's perception of De Campo as a self-satisfied, traditional brand. How was he going to dispel that if she wouldn't even look at his research? Sending her to visit Gabriele in Napa might be the only way. She was as stubborn as Matteo was. And as closed a book as he'd ever seen. You might manage to penetrate those outer layers, but she was never going to let you any further in than that.

Exhaling deeply, he pushed away from the window and climbed the stairs to his room. He needed sleep. But his mind, as he folded himself into bed, was wide-awake. The anniversary of Giancarlo's death was just days away. His role in that tragedy haunted him every waking hour of his life. Made it impossible to forget. So he focused on that utterly beddable version of Quinn standing outside her room instead. Anything not to go there.

He was now convinced Julian Edwards was a fool. That he couldn't have been man enough for his wife. Because if that'd been him, if he'd had Quinn in his bed, she wouldn't have been going anywhere.

He didn't need to know what it would be like to taste her. He'd already done it in his head.

Quinn woke with a massive headache and a severe desire to avoid snorting, four-legged beasts who could accidentally crush you with a misplaced step. Also a particular two-legged variety whose name started with Matteo and ended with De Campo.

Unfortunately avoidance was not an acceptable strategy, so two aspirin and two cups of Maria's strong black Tuscan coffee would have to do for the headache. As for the beast part? Both versions looked disgustingly fresh and beautiful in the dewy morning air, a jeans-clad Matteo in a navy T-shirt, his dark hair still damp from the shower, making a mockery of 99 percent of the world's male population in casual attire. He was holding the reins of a dark brown mare with elegant long legs, certainly of aristocratic heritage.

Quinn stood there, head throbbing, staring dubiously at them both.

"I'd really rather go on foot."

"She is irreproachably lovely," Matteo countered. "You'll be fine."

He held the stirrup out. She took a tentative step toward the horse. Jumped as the mare snorted and blew out a breath, sending a puff of steam snaking through the air. She pressed a hand to her pounding heart. Matteo's mouth curved. "You had a bad experience with a horse?"

She nodded. "One bolted on me as a child. I've been too afraid to ride since."

"Someone should have gotten you back in the saddle right away. That's the key."

"They tried. I wouldn't do it." She shifted her weight to both feet and exhaled slowly. "Really, I'd rather walk."

"Quinn." There was no mistaking the command in his voice. "You cannot miss out on this experience for the rest of your life because you're scared. I've never seen Marica bolt on someone. *Ever.*"

She sliced him the sharpest of looks. "I'm not stupid. Anything can make a horse shy and bolt. Even the nicest animal in the world, which I'm sure she is."

"And here I did not take you for a quitter," he taunted, eyes flashing. "Fine." He gathered up the reins. "I'll take the horses back to the stable and we'll take the car."

Humiliation seared through her as he started to lead the

mare away. She wasn't a quitter. She wasn't ever a quitter. *Damn him.*

"Okay, fine." He stopped and turned around. "I'll do it. But so help me God if she bolts on me I will make you pay."

His gray eyes crinkled at the corners. "How...thought provoking. You have a deal, Quinn Davis."

He led the horse back to her. The inquisitive mare cocked her ears and budged Quinn's arm with her nose. Her heart slammed into her chest. God help her. This was so not right.

Matteo held the stirrup out for her. "I'll be here beside you every step of the way."

That was not supercomforting. Not after last night. Not after she'd pretty much thrown herself at him and he'd walked away. She pressed her lips together and slid the ball of her foot into the stirrup. Hoisted herself up. Mounting a horse wasn't nearly as easy as it looked and her lack of momentum would have sent her back to the ground if Matteo hadn't planted a firm hand on her denim-clad behind and pushed her into the saddle.

Heat flooded her face as she sank her hips down into the leather. "Thank you."

"Mounting's the hardest part," he came back, deadpan.

She picked up the reins and focused on the terrifying beast rather than on Matteo's double entendres. She had no doubt he could dish them out all day and night.

He swung into the saddle of his very big, very dangerous-looking stallion with a lithe movement.

"What's his name?" she gibed. "Lucifer?"

His eyes gleamed with laughter. "Anteros, after the Italian god of love and passion. Perfect for me, don't you think?"

"Utterly."

His smile widened. "*Andiamo.* Let's go."

He went first on the big stallion, leading the way down

the narrow dirt road that wound its way through the mountain. True to his word, Marica followed quietly, picking her dainty way down the path. Quinn's heartbeat slowed as she took in the lush green hills dotted with the most exquisitely colored wildflowers. The rows upon rows of perfectly straight, perfectly groomed vines. Matteo pointed out the different crops at each elevation, detailing the ideal growing conditions for each varietal and why.

When the sun had risen high in the sky, they took a break for lunch in the winery. Matteo and his master winemaker took her through the complex techniques they used to produce some of the world's most exquisite wines. Then it was back on horseback to explore the other side of the mountain where the prize Brunellos and Chiantis were cultivated.

They finished the tour high up on the mountain as the sun was setting, a fiery red ball sinking behind the hills. Quinn pulled her mare to a halt behind Anteros, so glad she had taken the challenge and gone on horseback. The view would not have been nearly the same in a Jeep. Would not have allowed her to truly appreciate the beauty and scale of the massive historic vineyard.

She leaned over and patted the mare's silky neck, feeling rather victorious at conquering her fear. The sun and fresh air had cleared the throb in her head and chased away her jet lag.

"You really are lovely," she murmured. The mare's ears pricked up as if to say, *yes, I know.*

Matteo dismounted, tethered his horse and came to stand beside her. A smile curved his lips. "Feeling braver?"

She shrugged. "You were right. She's wonderful."

"She is."

She slid her feet out of the stirrups. Her legs felt like limp spaghetti, her butt so numb she couldn't feel it anymore. "Walking might be an issue," she murmured.

"Why do you think I'm standing here?" He held out his hands. "Come."

Why that command made her heartbeat increase by about ten beats per second was beyond her. She swung her leg over the saddle and let him lift her down. He kept his hands around her waist as he had last night to steady her, except this time she hadn't consumed a bottle of wine and she had her wits about her. Not that that seemed to help. His earthy, male scent was even more intoxicating than the aftershave he'd had on the night before. The hard strength of his arms around her equally so. Maybe it was just the general Matteo effect, she admitted, pulling in a steadying breath. Because he was more male than any man she'd met in her life. Hands down.

She stepped back and made herself busy spreading the blanket he handed her on the grass. If she didn't look at all the maleness and certainly if she didn't touch it, she could keep this under control.

Right?

Matteo took a bottle of De Campo's prizewinning champagne out of the saddlebags, along with glasses and a Swiss Army knife. Quinn gave him a wry glance as she eased her sore body down on the blanket. "Not too much for me."

"You can't enjoy this view without at least a taste." He handed her the glasses and deftly opened the bottle. "It's a tradition."

The sparkling liquid he poured into their glasses was the palest of golden yellows. The blanket seemed to shrink to miniscule proportions as he folded himself down beside her and handed her a glass. She eased toward the opposite edge in a subtle movement. The corners of Matteo's mouth lifted. "I'm hogging," she offered in an offhand tone.

"Mmm," he nodded. "You and your huge surface mass."

She couldn't help her smile. She unleashed it so infrequently these days it felt good to get it out. "Thank you for today," she said, tipping her glass toward him. "I'm glad you convinced me to do it on horseback. It was amazing."

"Prego." He lifted his glass. *"Salute."*

She tipped the liquid into her mouth. The tiny bubbles exploded on her tongue like the most potent ambrosia. Wow. She wasn't normally a huge fan of champagne or any sparkling wine for that matter, but this was dry and tart and perfectly balanced.

Matteo sat back on his elbows. "So tell me about our trip to St. Lucia. What are we going to see?"

She drew her knees up to her chest and wrapped her arms around them, letting her glass dangle from her fingers. "We have two hotels on the island. They'll allow you to see the two sides of Luxe, one of our jewels, and one of our properties that needs a lot of work. Paradis Entre les Montagnes near the island's famous twin volcanoes has been ranked one of the world's top five luxury hotels. Our chef there is top-notch, the menu ready to go for the wine pairings. Le Belle Bleu, on the north end of the island, is about to reopen after an extensive renovation. It's a work in progress. The menus haven't been finalized yet. But all the more reason for you to meet with the chef and develop the pairings from the ground up."

He plied her with questions as they drank their champagne. Lifted the bottle in question when she finished her half glass.

"No...thank you," she murmured dryly. "But I am sold. On all of it." She waved her hand at the vineyard and *castello* spread out in front of them in all its magnificence. "You must be so proud to be part of such history."

He nodded. "I'm incredibly privileged to be a De Campo. Absolutely."

She heard a hesitation in his voice. "But?"

He shrugged and looked down at the *castello,* sparkling

like golden fire in the dying rays of the sun. "Being a De Campo can be a challenge."

"Your father is difficult." Which was putting Antonio De Campo's legendary reputation mildly.

His mouth twisted. "He's a titan. I'm sure you can relate."

"Ah yes. I wonder what would happen if we put Antonio and Warren in the ring together? Who would win?"

His smile deepened. "I'd be fascinated to see."

"Did you all choose the family business or was it expected of you?"

"There was no choice. We are De Campos."

Sounded familiar. "Didn't Riccardo race cars for a while?"

"Si." He took a long swallow of his wine. "My father made it hell for him when he came back."

"Why *did* he come back?"

"Antonio was ill. He wanted Riccardo to take the reins."

She threw him a curious look. "What would you have been if you hadn't been a De Campo then? If you could have chosen?"

He arched a dark brow at her. "Is this an attempt to peer into my psyche? Part of your partner personality analysis?"

She smiled. "Answer the question."

"I would have been a concert pianist."

Her jaw dropped. "Seriously?"

He lifted a shoulder. "I'm not half bad. I minored in music at Oxford."

Those hands. Her gaze slid to their elegant length. She yanked it back with effort. *Oh, no, you don't, Quinn. Don't you dare start getting fascinated.*

"And you?" He waved a hand at her. "What would you have been if not a high-ranking executive?"

"I don't know," she said honestly. "I've never stopped to think about it. From the minute Warren saw me make scads of money with a lemonade stand, there was never any question of my path."

His mouth tipped up at the corner. "How did Thea end up, of all things, a veterinarian?"

"She was hopeless with numbers. It was just never going to happen. Warren gave up."

"And you filled the gap." He slid her a sideways look. "You seem very different, you two."

She lifted her shoulders. "I'm adopted. Not surprising."

"How did my intelligence miss *that?*"

"It's not something we talk about publicly. Warren and Sile adopted me when I was less than a year old."

"Do you know who your birth parents are?"

She nodded. "They live in Mississippi. They weren't able to keep me."

Something in her voice must have alerted him to the wealth of emotion beneath the surface. His gaze rested on her, but he didn't push. "You and Thea seem close despite the differences."

"We are." She smiled. "Thea is the one who believes in fairy tales. I'm the cynic always waiting for the penny to drop. We balance each other out."

"Does the penny always drop?"

She stared down at the glowing *castello.* "Sometimes it does."

He studied her for a long moment. "My brothers and I are very different too. But close as well. Riccardo likes to rule the world. Gabriele is obsessed with his wine."

"And you?"

"I'm not sure I want a label. Care to give me one?"

Undeniably sexy. Broodily magnetic? There were just so many. She shook her head. Safer that way.

"Do you play the piano for others?"

"Not usually no."

"Do you take requests to do so?"

"Are you asking?"

"Maybe." Dammit, yes she was curious, so curious to see how those beautiful hands worked a piano.

It was better than imagining them carrying out the slow and easy seduction of a woman. Something she was definitely, absolutely never going to experience.

His gaze turned an incendiary gray. "How about I play for you when De Campo wins the pitch?"

Her heart tripped over itself. "Gambling again..."

"Gambling is a miscalculation." He levered himself up off his elbows. "Like me betting on the fact that you don't want me to kiss you right now when you absolutely do."

"I don't," she whispered, her palms going sweaty as he leaned toward her.

"Liar," he murmured, cupping her jaw in his fingers, his gaze locked on hers. "You wanted me to kiss you last night and you want me to kiss you now."

"To which you did the smart thing and walked away," she protested weakly.

"Yes, but last night you'd had a bottle of wine. Tonight you're sober."

"Matteo—this is—"

"Just a kiss..." he murmured, bending his dark head toward her. She sucked in a breath, sure that wasn't going to be an adequate description. The slow, easy slide of his mouth across hers, as if he had all the time in the world, was so unlike the urgent, rough caresses Julian had always started with that it rocked her world. Then he did it again and again, until she was craving a firmer contact. Needing it. Her fingers curled into the soft jersey of his T-shirt, steadying herself, urging him on, she wasn't sure which.

He made a low sound under his breath, angled his mouth over hers and took the kiss deeper, exploring every centimeter of her lips with a sensual thoroughness that turned her into a mindless pile of flesh, his to command.

She had never known it could be like this—so deliciously intoxicating, so obviously meant to arouse and enjoy; not to dominate. Here on the top of the mountain, in a place like heaven, where nothing and no one else existed, she never wanted it to end.

"Matteo—" The word sounded so breathless and needy Quinn could hardly believe it was coming from her. He reached down, captured her hand and brought it to the back of his head. Invited her closer. The wiry coarseness of his hair beneath her fingertips was undeniably male, the teasing pressure of his tongue against the corner of her mouth tantalizing. She knew if she let him in it was going to be another mind-bending demonstration of what she'd been missing. But she did it anyway because she couldn't resist.

Big mistake. It was hot and never ending.

She never wanted it to end.

"Quinn."

The husky word pulled from Matteo's throat penetrated her consciousness with the force of a hammer. He dragged his lips across her cheek and rested his forehead against hers. "Now might be a good time to stop."

Stop? What was she doing?

She yanked her hand from around his neck and sat back, her palm covering her mouth. *Oh, my god.* She couldn't believe she'd just let him do that. That she'd participated in it. Eagerly.

Matteo's mouth flattened. "It was just a kiss, Quinn."

Just a kiss? She'd been necking with a man she could potentially award a ten-million-dollar contract to. If that wasn't a conflict of interest she wasn't sure what was!

Apparently he was starting to realize that too, because he'd whitened under that dark tan of his. "It won't happen again."

"You're damn right it won't happen again…" She jammed her palms against her temples. "We can't be kissing each other, Matteo. Despite your need to satisfy your curiosity with every woman on two legs."

He scowled. "That is not what that was."

"What was it then?"

He sighed. "A need to satisfy a curiosity specific to you, Quinn. And, a massive mistake, I agree."

She squashed the flutter that flickered to life in her stomach. Matteo rolled to his feet and held out a hand. "Your flight is early tomorrow. We should go."

She eyed the appendage warily, then took it. He pulled her up, stepping away from her as soon as she was level.

They didn't speak as they made their way down the mountain, the sky darkening into early dusk. Matteo led the way on Anteros, Marica following at a slow, steady pace. Quinn wished desperately for some of her mare's calm demeanor. Because that had not been her. She hadn't been able to let a man near her since Julian. Hadn't wanted to. Yet every time she got within five feet of Matteo De Campo she wanted his hands all over her.

Matteo De Campo. She wasn't sure if she should be thrilled she wasn't the ice queen everyone, including herself, thought she was or distraught at her incredibly bad judgment.

Her mouth compressed. Matteo was playing a game. He was playing to win. And she was acting like some silly pawn in it. She clenched her legs around Marica as they went down a steep section, her muscles crying out at the request. Crazy when she had a to-do list as long as her arm of major do-or-die issues she needed to take care of with Luxe.

She needed to get on that plane tomorrow morning with her head on straight, primed for what lay ahead.

Put temptation out of reach.

Unfortunately, her track record of late wasn't stellar.

CHAPTER FIVE

MATTEO HAD KNOWN he was going to kiss Quinn from the moment she'd gotten down off Marica, her green eyes glowing with the exhilaration of having conquered her fear. Most definitely after he'd heard the intense vulnerability in her voice when she'd said her birth parents hadn't been able to keep her. He'd taken action after one too many not-so-subtle invitations from the queen of mixed signals, and the result had been a scientific experiment gone horrifically right. A chemistry test he wished he could forget, but had been burned into his brain ever since Quinn had left Italy two days ago.

Not even the mountain of work he'd plowed through on the ten-hour flight to St. Lucia had been enough to banish the memory of an eager, passionate Quinn in his arms. The fact that she'd answered his question about what she'd be like when she totally let go hadn't put his curiosity to rest. It had made it much, much worse. Because now he knew.

His low curse was drowned out by the roar of the surf below the dramatic, open wall of his suite at Paradis Entre les Montagnes, Luxe's world-renowned luxury resort tucked between the island's famous twin volcanoes. He straightened his bow tie in the mirror and scowled. Why in God's name hadn't he just packaged up the insight he'd gained from digging into her hard-to-penetrate psyche and used it to work her angles? Why had he had to *kiss* her?

He picked his jacket up and shrugged it on with an antagonized movement. Bad judgment seemed to be his specialty. No matter how many times he told himself Angelique Fontaine had pursued him that night in Paris, had followed him to his hotel room after his drinks with his brothers and thrown herself at him, it had been *his* huge error to let her in. His shortsightedness to medicate himself with a woman intimately involved with a deal that could make De Campo's future.

His breath came out in a long hiss. Things might not always have been perfect in his family, but they were everything to each other. Family was everything. He had to find a way to rid himself of that little demon that sat on his shoulder urging him to do all the wrong things. Because the Luxe deal was his chance to rebuild his reputation with his brothers. To right his past mistakes. And he wasn't screwing it up.

A glance at the clock told him he had five minutes before he met the others. He strode out to the edge of the patio with its mind-blowing view of the volcanoes, wrapped his fingers around the iron railing and tried to find the focus that usually came so easily to him. Tucked into the mountains directly across from the spectacular peaks, Paradis Entre les Montagnes—literally translated as Paradise Between the Mountains—had proven to be as beautiful as its namesake. A lush, green haven perched above the Caribbean Sea, it disappeared into the mountainside with its tropical hardwoods, stone and tile chosen to blend in with its surroundings.

He moved his gaze over the layered blues of the Caribbean Sea that sparkled at the bottom of the cliff, over the tropical flowers of every hue and variety that bathed the resort in a jumble of color. The two mighty volcanoes loomed over it all, a vivid reminder of the power of nature. They were, apparently, still active. What would it be like if they roared back to life? Would they match the combustive feeling inside of him? Like he was ready to blow...

He shook his arms and legs out, the long flight from Italy leaving him stiff and sluggish. His head throbbed with that low, insistent pulse that had been with him all day. The three-year anniversary of Giancarlo's death was tomorrow. And as usual, nothing or no one had been able to wipe it from his mind.

Three years ago his best friend had perished because of a stupid bet. His bet.

It rested just below the surface, ready to push Matteo into inconsolability whenever he began to feel a measure of peace. Had been the driving force of every mistake he'd made since. Had driven his frenzied partying and out of control lifestyle until he'd shut it all down.

Without that oblivion, he felt like a man with enough burning lava inside of him to destroy an entire civilization.

He braced his hands against the railing and looked out over the water. A desert island would be preferable right about now. Instead, he had a manager's cocktail party to attend with Quinn and Daniel. A head chef and sommelier to win over. Perhaps a good thing since drinking himself into a stupor was no longer an option.

Something else he had banned from his life.

He clenched his hands by his sides. He would do this like he always did. By pretending to the world he didn't care. By being Matteo the Charming. Matteo who lit up a room when he walked into it. It was like switching on a lightbulb. Declaring it showtime.

The sky was transforming into a potent cocktail of pink and orange as he took the path down to the terrace that overlooked the sea. A small group of exquisitely dressed men and women chosen to enjoy cocktails with the manager sipped champagne in the sultry tropical air that still steamed from the heat of the day, a calypso band lending a distinctly West Indian flavor to the party. He stopped at the edge of the crowd and took in the scene. Daniel Williams was schmoozing the resort's manager, Thomas Golding, with that same smarmy smile he seemed to have constantly painted across his face.

Margarite, Quinn's head sommelier from New York, looked cool and elegant in a sleek royal-blue dress as she spoke with Paradis's head chef, François Marin, Quinn and a tall, distinguished-looking male in his early fifties. The gray-haired man's attention was riveted on Quinn. Matteo didn't blame him. Margarite had French chic, but Quinn looked…drool-inducing.

Gone was the conservative style of dress he was used to. In its place was a figure-hugging fuchsia sheath with a slit up the side just far enough to make a man look twice. Spaghetti straps made a mockery of the gravity required to wear the dress, because it was not the straps holding it up, it was the full-on perfection of Quinn's voluptuous curves that was doing it.

Damn. His mouth went dry. Why choose now, after that kiss, to pull out this new weapon in her arsenal? She'd even left all of that soft, silky hair down, sliding against the bare skin of her back. It took very little imagination to picture it spread across the ivory silk sheets of his suite's king-size bed. Less still to picture himself picking up where that kiss had left off, indulging the urge to explore every inch of her creamy flesh.

He shut the fantasy down in the middle of its full glory and grabbed a glass of champagne off a passing waiter's tray. *Get a goddamned handle on yourself, De Campo.* To-night was the night he was going to master the devil inside of him. Not let it loose.

Work the room. Get François Marin and Margarite Bellamy on your side. And then get out.

* * *

Quinn told herself the dress was absolutely appropriate as she watched Matteo's jaw hit the ground. She hadn't had time to shop for the sweltering St. Lucian temperatures before she'd left Chicago, so she'd turned herself over to Manon in the hotel's boutique to outfit her with a few dresses. Manon had assured her this soft, gorgeous designer dress in the finest silk was perfect for the cocktail party, but Quinn had felt it clung far too much.

She was now sure of it.

She smoothed the silky material over her hips and gave him her most professional smile. Margarite caught the nervous movement, her gaze sweeping over her. "So what's with the dress? You never wear anything like that."

"New addition to my wardrobe," she muttered.

Margarite's thin mouth quirked upward. "I heard François say it was a definite improvement."

Quinn bristled. "He did?"

"He's a French male, Quinn. By the way, he's right. You should play up your natural assets, not hide them."

Quinn wasn't sure what to do with that so she pushed her hair out of her face and directed a glance at the hottest man in the room. "I should introduce you to Matteo."

"Oh, I don't need an introduction." Her blonde, very young, very talented sommelier's blue eyes glittered. "I met him on the beach earlier. He had the whole place in an uproar. It's cruel and unusual punishment making me do business with him, Quinn."

She wasn't the only one. Quinn had the distinct feeling the sight of Matteo De Campo in swim trunks would be as impossible to eradicate from her memory as that kiss.

"He brought me a bottle of the Brunello," Margarite crowed. "Too bad I can't invite him back to my suite to share it with me."

Quinn shot her a look that told her what she thought of

that. Margarite waved a hand at her. "God, you've got to loosen up and learn how to take a joke, Quinn."

She bit down on her lip. Another of Julian's complaints about her. How dull and uninspiring a wife she'd turned out to be.

"Focus on business," she said shortly. "You wanted to be a part of this process. Make the best decision for Luxe."

Quinn started across the room toward Matteo, her sommelier trailing after her, a bemused look on her face. She knew she came across like a bitch sometimes but that's what happened when your husband verbally abused you for a year. You shut down. You just didn't care.

Whatever electricity she'd sensed between her and Matteo was nowhere in sight as he bent down to kiss her on both cheeks. He looked focused, all business, and kept his gaze on Margarite as he grilled her with questions, interspersed with enough charm that her sommelier just kept spilling the goods. Why that hurt her feelings she didn't know. She should be *glad* he seemed to be taking their agreement seriously.

Except there was a part of her that had come alive with him on that mountain. That kiss had blown her perception of herself apart—made her wonder exactly who she was. Because not once had she ever kissed her husband like that. Or wanted to for that matter.

Was she Quinn the ice queen or Quinn, a woman capable of more?

She blinked and gave her head a shake. That was all inconsequential right now. Why was she devoting even a tenth of her brain to her ill-advised attraction to a playboy she couldn't have anything to do with when she had at least two hours of paperwork to do after this cocktail party and a report to give to her father? She ought to be taking a page out of Matteo's book and not going there.

They finished their cocktails and sat down to dinner

on the outdoor terrace with François, Margarite, Daniel and Thomas Golding. There was no lack of conversation at the table of extroverts as the sun slid down behind the mountains and dusk settled over the island. Daniel was his usual smooth, conversational self, regaling them with his tall tales from the Outback; François, with his equally tall tales from the kitchens of Paris. Matteo won the chef and Margarite over with his charm and extensive knowledge of the hospitality and wine industries. But there was an edge to him tonight she couldn't put a finger on. A tension to his demeanor that took her back to that night in the cellar.

"Quinn tells me we'll get to explore the kitchens tomorrow and see the new menus you have planned," Matteo said to François. "I'm very much looking forward to it."

"*Oui,* in the morning." The chef nodded. "In the afternoon we must prepare for the celebrity chef challenge we're hosting."

"Every year we host a prestigious competition amongst all the chefs on the island to raise money for the schools here," Margarite explained. She nodded toward Matteo. "François is down a sous chef. Didn't you say you trained with Henry Thiboult in New York?"

Matteo inclined his head. "Not really formal training. I like to cook. He was kind enough to let me work in the kitchen with him a few times."

Quinn's mouth dropped open. "When in the world did you have time to do that?"

He let loose one of those flirtatious smiles she hadn't seen much of this evening. "Here and there. I told you I liked to cook."

François's sun-aged face split in a wide smile. "Anyone who has trained in Henry's kitchen is welcome in mine."

Margarite arched a brow at Matteo. "Are you up for it?"

"I'd be honored. As long as you don't mind my amateurism."

The chef beamed. "*Mais, oui*. I need you. It's all set then."

Daniel Williams looked dumbfounded. "I'd like to do it, too, then."

François looked down his nose at him. "Do you have any training?"

"Well, no, but—"

"So sorry." François waved a hand at him. "Only trained chefs in my kitchen. You'll cut off a finger and I'll lose my license."

A pout twisted Daniel's lips, if that was possible for a man. He sat and watched Matteo talk about working in Henry's kitchen, the famous Manhattan chef notorious for his culinary theatrics. François's booming laughter lit up the night. By the time dinner had stretched past the two-hour mark, Daniel Williams was distinctly red in the face.

"I hear De Campo's expanding into Chicago next year." The Silver Kangaroo CEO picked up his beer and took a sip. "Y'all are doing great. Next thing you know you'll be pushing that top-chef guy right out on his skinny behind."

"I hope so," Matteo agreed evenly. "We are focused on that very niche segment of the market."

Daniel shrugged. "You're making a lot of money in the restaurant business. Can't imagine De Campo's going to stop there."

"But we are." Matteo set down his beer, his gaze locked on his opposition. "Organizations that spread themselves too thin ultimately fail. You should know that, Williams. Your first venture collapsed, didn't it?"

Daniel flinched. "I consider that a war wound. Gotta take the hard knocks to get where you're going."

Matteo shrugged. "From what I've heard, poor management was to blame."

And the gloves were off. Quinn set down her coffee cup. "Perhaps we should call it a night. We have an early start tomorrow."

"I think I'd like an after-dinner drink," Daniel interjected, a belligerent tilt to his chin. "Care to join me, De Campo?"

Matteo started to decline, but Margarite jumped in. "We have some amazing ports at the bar. Let's have one then call it a night."

What was she doing? Quinn shot Margarite a warning look, but the other woman was already standing up, smiling at Matteo. Quinn set her mouth in a grim line. One drink and they were breaking this up.

At the bar near the cascading waterfall, she tried to slide onto the empty stool beside Matteo, intent on keeping the two men apart, but Daniel beat her to it. She took the one on the other side of the Australian while Margarite moved behind the bar and started picking out the ports.

"I might have something harder," Daniel drawled. "How about some Armagnac?"

"Sure." Margarite plucked the bottle out. "Matteo?"

"Not for me, *grazie*. The port is fine."

The rough, uneven tone of his voice drew Quinn's gaze. She stared at his face. His tanned skin had lost all its color, his gray eyes vacant.

"Oh, come on, De Campo," Williams boomed. "Be a man. Have one with me."

"I said no."

Three set of eyes gaped as Matteo stood up. "I'm going to turn in. Good night."

He was gone before Quinn had a chance to register what had happened. Margarite frowned. "Is he okay?"

No, he was not. He was far from okay. Heart pounding, Quinn stood up. "I'll go check on him. You two enjoy your drink."

* * *

In his suite, Matteo pulled off his jacket and the tie that threatened to choke him. Yanked the top buttons of his shirt loose. He stared at the bottles of the fully stocked bar for a long moment, the heated rush of a hard shot calling to him like a siren's song. Then jerked away. The keys of the grand piano in his suite, undoubtedly Quinn's idea, would normally have beckoned but he was too far gone even for that.

He kicked his shoes and socks off and walked down to the private beach. Strode through the powdery white sand to the water's edge. Giancarlo had been drinking cognac the night of the accident. That big smile of his on full display, his friend had slapped him on the back and gestured for the bartender. *"Come on, De Campo, let's close it off with the good stuff. A perfect drink to end a perfect night."*

He could have saved things right there. Instead he had gone along with the insanity. Fed his best friend's death wish.

The contents of his stomach rose up to the back of his mouth. *Why didn't you stop it? You were supposed to be the sensible one.*

Or had he had his own death wish?

"Matteo."

Quinn's voice penetrated his haze. He stayed where he was, his back to her, because he didn't want her to see him like this. Didn't want anyone to see him like this.

"I'm fine. Go back to the others."

"You aren't fine. You haven't been fine all night. What happened back there?"

He turned around. "It was nothing," he said harshly. "Go back to the others."

She crossed her arms over her chest. "I'm not leaving until you tell me. You look like you've seen a ghost."

A harsh bark of laughter escaped him. "I have."

She stepped closer, her gaze on his face. "This is about Giancarlo."

"Dammit, Quinn. Go."

"What happened with him? You are clearly not okay, Matteo."

Frustration erupted like a spew of volcanic ash. Rose up inside him like an unstoppable force, curling his hands into fists at his sides, sending his breath flaming through his nostrils. "It's the anniversary of his death tomorrow. It's a bad night for me, that's all."

"Oh." She pushed her hair out of her face, her beautiful eyes gleaming with compassion. "I'm so sorry. How long has it been?"

"Three years," he said bleakly. Three years of hell.

She stepped closer, her fingers curving around his forearm. "Do you want to talk about it?"

"One kiss does not make a confessional," he rasped, jerking away. "The only thing that makes this better is alcohol or a woman, Quinn, and since I've sworn off the former as a source of anesthesia and we've agreed you are off-limits, you need to walk away."

She stared up at him, her hazel eyes huge. "I don't think... I don't want to leave you like this..."

"Walk, Quinn." Close to the edge and terrified of her seeing him go over it, he reached up and brushed his fingers across her cheek. "I'm doing my best to keep this strictly business. But you in that dress tonight isn't anything about business. All I can think about is stripping it off you and knocking my brain senseless because I know it would work." He ran his thumb down over her full, lush mouth. "I know you would blow my mind enough to pull me out of this. But we both know that can't happen. So leave...now."

Her mouth quivered under his thumb. She stood there and for a moment, he thought she might stay. Then she stepped back and did exactly what he'd known she would. Retreated. But her gaze remained firmly fixed on his face.

"I'm in the suite at the end of the road if you need someone to talk to. At any time, Matteo."

Then she turned and left.

He waited until she was out of earshot. Then he let out a primal yell the pounding surf swallowed up.

It was not nearly enough. It would never be enough.

CHAPTER SIX

WHEN A SLEEPLESS night had only made your brain more combustible, your balance on the high wire that was life more tenuous and your need to scream near deafening, you did whatever it took to make it through the day.

Fortunately for Matteo, working in François Marin's kitchen was an intense form of therapy that left no room for thought. A well-oiled machine, his kitchen ran with military precision, timed down to the minute, with no room for mistakes. Exactly what he needed right now on this darkest of days.

He had spent the morning touring the kitchens with François, Margarite, Daniel and Quinn, followed by an exhaustive study of the hotel's new menus. His knowledge of food and the unique wine pairings he'd suggested for François's menu had elicited an excited response from the chef. They fit perfectly with Quinn's eclectic vision and made Daniel Williams look like a neophyte in the process.

Exactly as planned. He sliced up a scallion with ruthless efficiency. After the menu review, much to Daniel William's chagrin, Matteo had joined the other sous chefs in the kitchen to prepare for tonight's chef's challenge. The guests weren't due until seven, but the preparation for this type of an event was massive. He alone had three sauces on the go and salads to plate.

Adrenaline pounded through his veins and fired his

movements as the clock ticked until he was a finely tuned cog in the machine, operating on command. He started on the hot peppers, tearing through them with a razor-sharp knife. If he moved from point A to point B to point C without deviating, he might, just might, not become unhinged.

Might forget that Quinn had seen into the deepest, darkest recesses of his mind last night. A place he'd never let anyone go.

Quinn tossed her pencil on the desk, sat back and rubbed her hands over her eyes. She'd finally gotten that report on her progress over to her father last night, but the rest of her paperwork and troubleshooting emails for the Mediterranean hotels had taken until well into the early hours. She was good at existing on six hours of sleep but anything less than that and she started to get distinctly unbalanced, her judgment skewed and unreliable.

Right now was a case in point. She should be working. Instead she couldn't get the haunted look on Matteo's face last night out of her head. The way he'd looked ready to tip over the edge. She'd had some tortured moments in her life, like the morning the private investigator had turned over that file on her parents and she'd found out the truth. That it had been her they hadn't wanted. But it hadn't come close to the look of pure agony on Matteo's face. Like he was being tortured by something beyond his control....

She frowned and steepled her fingers against the edge of the desk. Losing a best friend must be awful. She couldn't imagine losing Thea. But it had been three years since Giancarlo had died. Time enough to heal. So why was Matteo so tortured?

Picking up the pencil, Quinn pressed it against her temple. As if questioning her sanity. Because last night, even after Matteo had made it clear women were his anesthesia, that likely any woman would have done in that moment, she'd been tempted to stay. She could have said it had been her human side making a rare appearance. She was afraid it was a whole lot more than that.

She would check on him. Shoving her palms against the desk, she rolled to her feet. She'd stop by the kitchen, see how he was doing, then dress for the chef's challenge. Not that Thomas was going to need her help. Unlike his counterpart at Le Belle Bleu on the other side of the island, who apparently, from the paperwork, did not have everything running smoothly, Thomas was a genius at running a high-end establishment.

Quinn sighed. Tonight would be fun. Tomorrow, when they did their walk-through, she'd deal with Le Belle Bleu.

Taking a shortcut through the back of the hotel, she stepped into the kitchen. She'd seen grown men reduced to tears in François's pressure cooker of a production, but there was Matteo, working in a group of a half dozen sous chefs, looking like he'd spent his life there.

She watched, fascinated, as he pulled the pan half off the burner and tossed in four or five herbs. Was there anything the man couldn't do? And how had she ever pegged him a flirty playboy? He was a brilliant businessman. He also made chef's whites look outrageously good.

She stepped closer to see what the last sauce was. He gave her an even look. "Quinn."

"Just wondering what you're making," she said brightly. She pointed at the green sauce. "What's that?"

"An Indian mint sauce."

"Looks exotic."

"And I can't mess it up." He gave her a dark look. "You're not supposed to be in here."

"Just checking to see how you're doing."

He threw a couple of drops of hot sauce into the third sauce. "You're distracting me."

"How could I be distracting you? I've been here two seconds."

He gave her a deliberate once-over. "Do you really want to know?"

Heat burned a path up to her cheeks. "Not so much."

His eyes glittered. "François," he called out, pointing a finger at her. "She needs to go."

The chef quirked a finger at Quinn. "You know the rules. Out."

She gave Matteo an outraged look. "That was low, calling in the teacher."

He added the mushrooms to the hot sauce and shook the pan over the flame. "I want to win. Out."

Quinn turned around with a huff and left. He wanted to win because he wanted to make Daniel Williams look even more lackluster than he had this morning going through the menus. It had been painful to watch. He was rapidly shifting the tide and he knew it.

She got dressed and greeted the guests and judges with Thomas. The judges spanned everything from a native pop singer who'd made it big on the international music scene, to the prime minister and governor general of the island, to one of St. Lucia's most celebrated artists.

The evening went smoothly. Dinner was a gastronomic study in perfection, but it was François's main course—the lamb with Matteo's green mint sauce that stole the night. Quinn didn't even need to see a scorecard to know who had won it was so patently obvious from the looks on the judge's faces.

As the results were being tabulated, the chefs changed and came out to mingle with the crowd. She watched Matteo turn on the charm, drawing the VIPs to him like moths to a flame, including the St. Lucian pop singer, Catrina James, who was beautiful and vibrant in a fire-engine-red dress that showed off her creamy, perfect skin. Quinn had never seen such a chameleon as Matteo. He molded himself into exactly what he needed to be at any given moment. Brilliantly.

He had changed into gray pants and a white shirt, his olive skin darker, swarthier from the hot rays of the Caribbean sun. It made his startling gray eyes stand out even more. Added to the intensity surrounding him, sitting just below the surface. Made him look even more dangerously attractive. If that was possible.

He caught her gaze. She pulled hers resolutely away and sat down at the bar, ordering herself a soda water. She'd been running all night, making sure things went smoothly. Sitting for a couple of minutes and reviewing the itinerary the manager of Le Belle Bleu had sent over for their walk-through tomorrow would be a beautiful thing the way her feet ached.

Matteo slid onto the stool beside her just as the bartender delivered her soda water. The sexy scent of him drifted into her nostrils. Made it hard to concentrate.

"Would you like a drink?"

"*Si*. That kitchen was smoking hot."

Not the only smoking hot thing around here, her recalcitrant brain proclaimed. She ordered him the island beer he'd favored at dinner, and turned to him.

"You were brilliant in the kitchen. Is there anything you can't do?"

He gave her a thoughtful look. "I am hopeless under the hood of a car. Desperately bad at sudoku. And my grammar is sometimes suspect."

"Shameful."

"I wasn't blowing you off, Quinn. It was an act of self-preservation."

From what? Her stomach did a funny little jump. "How," she asked deliberately, "are you today?"

He pulled the beer the bartender set down toward him. "I'll be better tomorrow."

"Matteo—"

He held up a hand. "How about I ask you a question?"

Quinn surveyed him warily as he took a long swig of his beer. "All right."

He propped his elbow on the bar and rested his chin in his hand. "What was with the one-year marriage? Most people's exercise routines last longer than that."

She felt her face turn into fully petrified papier-mâché. "We were…incompatible."

He shook his head. "I'm not looking for the press release, Quinn. I'm looking for the truth."

"That is the truth." And a million other intricacies she couldn't even begin to get into.

Matteo looked at her for a long moment, those gunmetal-gray eyes of his seeming to look straight through her. "I think you were too strong a personality for him. He wasn't man enough to be with you."

She choked on the sip of wine she'd taken. "That's a big assumption coming from someone who doesn't know anything about it."

His eyes glittered. "I know you, Quinn. You aren't that hard to figure out."

She bit into the side of her mouth. "I think Julian would disagree," she said tightly. "He would tell you I was a boring workaholic who didn't know how to have fun."

"Then he'd be as much of a fool as I thought." His baldly stated words made her heart jump. "Any man with balls would recognize that for the lie it is. There isn't any part of you that could ever be described as boring, Quinn. As anything but full-on fascinating."

A flush of warmth swept through her. "You don't have to feed me compliments, Matteo. I have thick skin."

"Then you can take me telling you the truth." He let the

loaded statement sit on the air until he was sure he had her full attention. "If we were doing anything but negotiating a ten-million-dollar deal right now, we'd have been in bed together already. And I'd be taking apart the puzzle that is Quinn piece by piece." His gaze held hers, the intent behind it riveting. "I guarantee you I wouldn't be bored."

Her breath caught in her throat. Refused to continue on its way up to her brain where she needed it most.

"You are not a woman to be discarded," he said harshly. "He was a fool."

Quinn sat there speechless. Drowning in a new perspective that had never occurred to her before. Had Julian been intimidated by her? Had he tried to hurt her, humiliate her to make himself feel like more of a man? Because she'd been too much of one?

Her world tilted on its axis. Fractured apart as a seismic shift ripped the ground from beneath her feet and set her adrift. She'd spent the past year torturing herself with ways she could have saved her marriage. Ways she could have changed to keep her husband from straying. Allowed her self-confidence to be completely ripped apart when he'd found her wanting every time. When in reality, maybe her marriage had been destined for failure from the start. Because of the man Julian was. Who they both were.

One of the chefs came over and grabbed Matteo for the winner's announcement. Quinn sat there, head buzzing as she watched him walk away. She had always believed that at the heart of her, she was somehow defective. Her disastrous marriage had only underscored it. *What if it wasn't true*? What if her inability to please her husband in bed had been more about him than her?

With her belief about her biggest failure turned upside down, she stood at Thomas Golding's side as they announced the winner of the chef's challenge. Paradis, to no one's surprise, won, François's lamb dish and outrageously eclectic-green banana pie outclassing the competition by a landslide.

Catrina James presented François with the winner's trophy and gave each of the chefs a kiss on the cheek as she posed with them for photographs. Her one for Matteo was extra enthusiastic. *Of course.*

Champagne bottles were popped and the night dissolved into a big party. It was impossible not to get caught up in the exuberant celebrations, but as she watched, as the clock slipped closer to midnight, Matteo's easy smile faded. His face shuttered and the darkness descended. It was like watching a curtain fall and she knew he'd been hiding his pain under that charming, devil-may-care demeanor.

Tonight was the anniversary of Giancarlo's death.

It did not surprise her to turn around sometime after midnight to find Catrina James attached to another male and Matteo gone. She stood at Thomas Golding's side, the ground feeling unsteady under her feet. She should go back to her room and work. She had enough of it for an army.

Matteo was a conflict of interest in the most important assignment of her career. She should be running in the opposite direction. But some things in life were more important than work. Funny how she'd realized that now of all moments.

Quinn looked down at the golden shimmer of the Riesling in her glass, the sparkling liquid reflecting the light of the moon. *I know you would blow my mind enough to pull me out of this....*

Her heartbeat picked up into an insistent rhythm that made the blood whish in her ears. How could any deal matter when a person was in agony? She could not leave Matteo alone. She would not.

She could not spend another minute of her life wondering about the truth of herself.

"Excuse me," she murmured to Thomas. "I have some work to do."

Crossing the terrace, she took the path to the upper level of luxury suites. Saw the light burning in Matteo's living room. She climbed the steps to the door and was about to rap on it when she heard music. A haunting piano score played so beautifully it froze her in her tracks.

Matteo.

Her heart pounded so loud in her chest she thought it might break through. She knew she was invading his privacy. Knew she should walk away. But the melody reached out and wrapped itself around her heart. The blackness of it.

Quinn walked around to the back of the suite and took the stairs up to the patio. Leaned back against the wall in the shadows and listened to every heartrending note. She did not recognize the piece, but there was no doubt in her mind Matteo had written it for Giancarlo. It was poignant, stunning and full of grief.

Her knees shook, her eyes burned. She was not someone made of emotion. But this was breaking her heart.

She wasn't sure how long she stood there, pressed against the wall, listening to him play. When he finally stopped, she took a deep breath, steadied herself and stepped into the light. He sat at the piano staring at the keys. He looked up as she appeared, as if he wasn't at all surprised to find her there. His bloodshot eyes were nearly her undoing.

"I told you last night you can't help." His voice was gritty, broken. "This is my personal forty-eight hours of hell, Quinn. Leave me to it."

She shook her head. "Whatever this is, whatever happened to Giancarlo, you have to let it go. You can't keep doing this to yourself."

He looked down at the keys, his back ramrod straight. "You should go."

Her stomach convulsed in a long pull. She looked down at the threshold that divided the patio from the inside space. Made her choice.

He looked up as she walked into the room. "Quinn—"

She sat down on the stool beside him and took his face in her hands. "You have to make it stop," she told him huskily. "I know what it's like to keep your demons inside. To let them torture you. You will destroy yourself."

He pulled her hands away, the desperate, hopeless look in his eyes of a man who'd suffered too much. "I can't. Dammit, I can't."

She sank her palms into the hard line of his jaw. "Then help me chase our demons away together."

He went completely still, his gaze holding hers. "What are you saying?"

She swallowed hard, fighting the part of her that wanted to run because that was what she always did. "I need to know what you said to me earlier is true. That Julian was wrong about me."

The color seemed to leech from his skin. "You must know it's true."

"I don't," she said quietly. "I don't know anything. You said the other night that I could knock you out of this. Then use me. And let me prove him wrong about me."

Matteo shook his head, a desperate glitter in his eyes. "This is way over the line."

"I know. I just walked over it."

He rubbed his hands over his face. "The deal... I..."

"The deal doesn't exist tonight," she said harshly. "I am here and I am not leaving you."

He squeezed his eyes shut. "*Cristo.* Quinn..."

She sat there, heart slamming against her chest, terrified that he would reject her, that once again she would be deemed unacceptable. The silence hung between them like a loaded missile. When he opened his eyes, the anguish she saw there made her draw in a breath.

"I told you last night this is about numbing my mind. You have to know that."

She wanted someone to numb hers. To make her forget she was Quinn Davis for just a few minutes. Make her feel alive again like she had on that mountainside.

His big body tensed beneath her hands, his breathing changed and became rough, fractured. "You're sure?"

She nodded. "One night. One night to make it go away for both of us."

Something shifted in his expression. A dark wildness moved within him. She drew in a breath as he slid a hand against her nape and brought his mouth down on hers. Her softness met his hardness in a caress that blew her mind right from the very first second. But unlike his kiss on the mountain, this one was hotter, all-consuming. Devouring and needy, it quickly descended into an urgent quest to pull her into the fire with him. Her fingers fisted against his chest in an involuntary reaction to a dominant male exerting his power over her. She flexed them against him. Forced herself to relax. *Dammit, Julian. You are not doing this to me. Not anymore.*

Matteo's scorching, openmouthed kisses drove the past from Quinn's head. He tasted her, licked into her until she could do nothing but focus on the heat they were generating. She pushed closer, met him kiss for kiss. And when that wasn't enough, he sank his hands into her waist, lifted her up and wrapped her legs around him, her bare skin sliding against the rough material of his trousers. The feel of his hard flesh beneath her made her heart slam against her chest. He was already aroused. Potently, highly aroused.

She wasn't sure she knew how to handle him.

Matteo pushed her back so he could look at her. Ran his

fingertips up her bare arms to her shoulders, his heated gaze sending goose bumps to every inch of her skin. Got her so caught up in him that was all she could think about. "You are the most beautiful woman I have ever seen," he murmured, sinking his teeth into her shoulder. "If you knew how close I was to breaking all the rules that night at the *castello*..."

She sucked in a breath. "You walked away..."

"I was one step away, Quinn. One."

She watched, hypnotized, as he slid his fingers under the straps of her dress and pulled them down. His muttered oath told her he appreciated the fact she'd had to lose her bra. His gaze as he cupped her hot, ultrasensitive flesh was reverent. "I'm a chest man," he murmured. "And yours..." he said, sliding his callused fingertips against the tips of her breasts, "is magnificent."

He held her gaze as his thumbs covered her nipples, circled them into erect, aching points. Her soft moan of pleasure made him take her mouth again in approval. "Talk to me, Quinn. Tell me what you like."

"More," she muttered. "Just...more."

He turned her around, pressed her back against the piano. The hard wood dug into her back, made her arch against it, but when he lowered his head and took her nipple into the heat of his mouth, she stopped caring. She dug her fingernails into his biceps and let out another low moan. He tugged, sucked and laved her until she was half-crazy with the pleasure of it. Feeling it deep down inside of her.

"You like that?"

"Yes."

He cupped her other breast in his hand and lavished the same treatment on it, tortured her with his swirling tongue until her insides collapsed and everything went liquid. She had never felt so needy, so desperate. So lost in something.

In him. Too shy to put it into words, she clamped her legs harder around him and begged with her body for more.

"Slow down," he murmured, pulling back. "We should take this to the bedroom."

She froze. "No bedrooms."

"No bedrooms?" He frowned down at her. "Why?"

"Here," she insisted. Moved her fingers to the buttons of his shirt. "I want you here."

A dark fire lit his gaze. He let her unbutton the shirt. Let her uncover his drop-dead gorgeous six-pack of a chest that was every bit as amazing as that of her ultrabuff Krav Maga instructor. Then he captured her hands at her sides. "I wasn't finished."

Her throat went dry. She was pretty sure she wanted him to finish. Positive actually.... He held her gaze as he spread her thighs wider, pushed her back firmer against the wood so that she was exposed to him. Vulnerable. Then he pushed the hem of her dress up her thighs in a deliberate motion that made her breath seize in her throat. His palms skimmed across her bare skin, branding her. "I thought you might have lost the panties too," he murmured, pressing the heel of his palm against the heat of her. "Not that I'm complaining. They're very sexy."

She sucked in a breath as he worked her with the heel of his hand. Her pleasure had never been of any consequence to Julian, it had been all about him. But Matteo was so focused, intent in the way he touched her. "You want more?" he asked, setting his mouth to the sensitive spot between her neck and shoulder.

"Yes." She moved her hips against him in an instinctive plea.

"Good," he murmured, sinking his hands into her waist and lifting her so her hips rested on the piano keys. "Because this is one fantasy I'm not denying myself."

He slid his hands under her dress, hooked his fingers

into the sides of her panties and made her lift her hips so he could strip them off. A bolt of excruciating self-consciousness sliced through her at the way she was displayed in front of him. Like an instrument for him to play.... But her heart was racing, the blood in her veins thrumming. The air sat heavy and humid around them, fragranced with a million exotic flowers. The only sound in the whisper-still night was the crash of the waves on the shore below. And it calmed her....

He kissed his way from the inside of her knees to the hot, pulsing core of her, taking her dress with him as he went. When she thought she might actually go mad for his touch, he worked his hands under her hips and lifted her to him. She jammed her hands into the keys on either side of her, the jarring sound of two opposite notes filling the air. It was raw and it was outrageous, but when he bent and put his mouth to her, she had never felt more perfectly connected to a person in her entire life. Like she was made for him to touch her like this.

Leisurely, exquisitely, he savored her, traced every nerve ending in a practiced seduction that drove her slowly, inexorably mad.

Her body tightened, her eyes flew wide. It had been impossible for her to orgasm with Julian. To perform on command. She had no idea what it felt like to experience it. But right now she felt as if her whole body was about to take flight. To soar into a place she'd never been before.

He flicked his tongue over the hard nub of her, took her there, then yanked her back. Again and again. She threw her head to the side. "God, please, I need—"

"Not yet," he rasped against her skin. "You can take more."

No, she couldn't. Not anymore. Then he slid a finger inside her and took her higher. Stroked her until he reached a spot that sent white-hot pleasure ratcheting through her.

Oh, my God. She jammed her palms into the keys. Sent another crazy symphony of sound bouncing off the walls. She was burning alive....

"Now," he ordered. "Now, Quinn."

He played the throbbing center of her with his tongue, expertly, urgently, his finger curving up inside her until the blinding heat made the blood roar in her ears. Then he took her over the edge, her scream of pleasure as he brought her to shuddering completion reverberated throughout the room.

On and on the pleasure coursed through her as he kept his mouth on her, drew out her orgasm, made her take it until her shaking body could handle no more and she pleaded for him to stop.

She was half-delirious when he picked her up and started toward the bedroom.

"Not there—"

He stared down at her. "What in *Dio's* name is wrong with a bedroom?"

She buried her face in his chest. "I just can't."

"What did he do to you, Quinn?" His voice was a low growl.

She shook her head and burrowed closer. "I don't want to talk about him."

He carried her to the silk embroidered sofa with the incomparable view of the Pitons and sat with her cradled against him. Lifted her chin with his fingers. "I knew it would be like that."

Her face burned. She had screamed, literally screamed for him.

His gaze was direct, steady. "You weren't like that with him."

"No."

She was acutely aware of his arousal, hard and unfulfilled beneath her. But her absolute inability to enjoy the sexual act in the past froze her in a purgatory of indecision. She wanted to give him as much pleasure as he'd given her. Wipe away the demons still blazing in his eyes.

But there were other ways to do it. And he made her feel beautiful and empowered enough to try. She sat up in his lap, framed his face with her hands and kissed him, the taste of herself on him so erotic it made her toes curl. His instant, heated response made her blood surge in her veins. "I'm not an expert at this," she whispered against his mouth. "So you need to tell me how I'm doing."

"Tell me," Matteo returned, his lips clinging to hers, "exactly what is it you're doing?"

She pressed her mouth to his hot, hard flesh as she worked her way down. "This."

Quinn took her time exploring him, learning him. It was so different to want to touch. To want to make him utter those soft sounds that told her she was doing it just right. To know she was doing it right. She sat back in his arms and brought her lips to his perfectly cut abs. Traced the dips and curves of his salty skin as she worshipped at the altar that was Matteo. When she reached the taut muscles of his abdomen, he tensed so completely she wondered if he was still breathing.

"You okay?"

His tortured *"eccellente"* made her smile.

"You want more?"

"You have no idea."

She slid the smooth leather free of his belt loop and undid it. Made swift work of his trouser button and zipper. He lifted his hips, helped her as she dragged his pants down over his long legs. Then there was nothing but a very virile, very aroused Matteo in black boxers staring her in the face. And her very, very dry mouth.

He was big. Bigger than Julian had been. The most perfectly put-together male she had ever seen. She wanted to touch him so badly her self-consciousness vaporized on a wave of lust.

His olive skin took on a ruddy hue as she sank to the floor in front of him, his gray eyes darkening to a sultry, mesmerizing slate. "This could have been another of my fantasies," he muttered as she lowered her mouth to the taut muscle just above the band of his briefs. Dragged her lips across the elastic band. "I'm going to give you the thumbs-up on that," he encouraged hoarsely, his big body stiffening beneath her, "but ask that you pick up the pace."

She slid her fingers into his boxers and sought him out. He was velvet soft over hard steel, so very masculine her breath caught in her throat. She wanted to learn this part of him too. To worship him as he'd worshipped her. To make him feel as desirable as she had.

She moved her hands over him, stroked him, explored him until he arched his hips toward her, his eyes tortured.

"Dammit, Quinn—more."

She lowered her head and took him into her mouth. Heard his guttural growl of approval. It was heady, empowering to be in control when she had never been in the past. Slowly at first, then faster she took him until he was covered in perspiration, until he was shaking beneath her, as out of control as she'd been. Until he couldn't be thinking about anything but what she was doing to him—just as she had. And the demons were banished.

Then she didn't hold back. His breathing fractured. His hands reached for her, tangled in her hair. "I want you with me."

Her stomach twisted, too many memories, too many humiliations filling her head. She pushed his hands away and took him deeper in her mouth. Increased her rhythm. His low curse filled the air. His hips jerked into her hands, his big body ready to explode.

"*Maledizione,* Quinn."

She lifted her head and watched as he caught himself with his hands and came with an explosive force that made her heart pound like a jackhammer.

Primal, erotic, beautiful. She was spellbound.

The room was silent except for the harsh force of his breathing. The weight of his gaze sat on her. Probing.

"I need to clean up," he muttered, rolling to his feet. "Do not move."

He came back in another pair of black boxers and drew her into his arms on the sofa. Set his lips to her hair. "When I said I wanted you to knock me senseless I didn't expect you to take it literally."

She laid her head against his chest. "I wanted it that way."

"I have condoms, you know."

"It wasn't about that."

He sighed. "You don't want to talk about it."

She shook her head and closed her eyes. For the first time in so long, she felt at peace. As if there wasn't a fractured part of her ready to disintegrate at any moment. She wanted to hold on to it. Savor it. Because it couldn't last. This had been one night. One night to get Matteo through the fire and one night to make her feel whole again. That's all it could be.

Minutes, hours passed. When she woke, Matteo's chest was moving slowly up and down beneath her cheek. The sky outside was pitch-dark, not a sound in the air.

She eased herself off him, looked down at his beautiful, hard-edged face. Shadows were painted beneath his eyes, making her wonder when the last time he'd slept well had been. But his jaw was relaxed, his body slack. He was peaceful now and she thought he would sleep for a long time.

Quinn walked silently to the piano, picked up her underwear and made herself walk out the door.

* * *

Matteo woke to flickering shadows. He blinked and sat up. Struggled to get his bearings. He was alone, the suite dark, the sky over the volcanoes just beginning to lighten.

Quinn's perfume lingered in the air. Her taste, her smell was all over him. Pieces of the night before stormed back, came together like puzzle parts. His near desperation. His struggle to rid himself of it at the piano. Quinn's appearance. The mind-blowing intimacies they'd shared...

The fact that he'd broken the one promise he'd made to his brother...

His stomach lurched. Yes, Quinn had needed this as much as he did; she'd had her own demons to slay. But it still didn't make it right. Nothing made it right.

A sheen of perspiration covered his body. Drove him to the fridge for water. He snatched out a bottle, twisted off the cap and tipped it into his mouth, the icy liquid chilling his throat like the most horrific of wake-up calls. He had slept with Quinn Davis. It would be impossible for him to believe he'd done it if she wasn't all over him. If the image of it wasn't so graphically implanted on his brain.

One night, she'd said. This has nothing to do with the deal.... Yet wasn't that exactly what Angelique Fontaine had promised just before she had destroyed him crying out her sorrows to her father?

His stomach dropped. What if Quinn couldn't handle what she'd done? What if she chose Silver Kangaroo because it was the only unbiased thing to do?

It occurred to him he might actually have a death wish. With a muffled curse he strode out onto the terrace. But the filtered light of early day only made his sins more blatantly clear. He raised his eyes to the rising sun and let it brand him with the truth. He had put his relationship with his family in jeopardy again over his inability to forget the past. To forgive himself for his trangressions.

He pressed his palms to his cheeks. Was it ever going to go away? Was he ever going to feel as if he deserved a place on this planet again when Giancarlo would never get to live out the best years of his life? Exactly how long was he going to punish himself? Destroy those around him?

Was there even any hope he ever would?

He thought about the trust Riccardo had put in him. Prayed his instincts were right and Quinn would not betray him. His chest tightened until it felt impossible to pull in air and everything went a hazy white.

He did not consciously register himself striding inside and pulling on swim trunks. Taking the stairs to the beach, walking straight into the water and setting out toward the volcanoes with powerful strokes.

Quinn had saved his soul last night. Now he had taken himself straight to hell.

CHAPTER SEVEN

"Say, was that De Campo I saw swimming across to the Pitons this morning?" Daniel Williams slopped half a cow's worth of milk into his coffee and looked across the breakfast table at Quinn. "I'm all off with my time zones and I sure as heck could have been seeing something, but I could swear I saw him out there and holy crow, that has to be some swim."

Quinn's spoon fell to her saucer with a clatter. "That can't be right." That swim was miles.

Daniel shrugged. "Like I said, I could be wrong but I thought I recognized him."

Her stomach tightened. Lord knew what state of mind Matteo had woken up in this morning. Sharks weren't a common worry in the waters here, but that was a bloody long swim. Even for a good athlete. He was supposed to have met them for breakfast a half hour ago before their trip to Le Belle Bleu…

She stood up abruptly. "I'm going to go see if he misunderstood the breakfast invitation. I'll meet you in the lobby in ten minutes."

She walked straight into Matteo as she exited the restaurant. Her heartbeat slowed to a more manageable rhythm as she took in his navy trousers, pale yellow shirt and the grim look he wore like a badge. At least he was in one piece.…

"Daniel said you'd swum across to the Pitons.... I told him he must have been mistaken."

"I did."

She stared at him. "That was exceedingly stupid."

"A skill I seem to be perfecting of late."

"Matteo—"

"Later, Quinn." His sharp tone stopped her in her tracks. "We need privacy for this discussion."

She bit into her lip. Or they could avoid it all together....

He waved a hand toward the restaurant. "I need coffee. I'll get one to take with us."

Matteo strode into the dining room, leaving Quinn standing there watching him go. She spent the windy drive around the coast to Le Belle Bleu trying to ignore the fact she'd just slept with the man behind her. Engaged in no-holds-barred raw sex with a man who had proven that far from her being the frigid, unfeeling creature Julian had made her out to be, she was capable of losing herself in the moment. As in screaming losing herself in the moment.

Images from the night before flashed through her head like a real-time movie she'd played a starring role in. Her spread across the piano keys...Matteo feasting on her willing body...

An allover flush consumed her. She wanted to feel regret. And she did. Sleeping with the bidder of an open contract likely wasn't spelled out in the Davis Investments ethics manual because they'd probably figured no one would ever go there. But if the board or Daniel Williams ever found out, there'd be hell to pay. Her judgment would be called into question and her reputation compromised.

Her head throbbed in her skull. The problem was she'd never felt so alive. Never knew she could. She had pulled Matteo back from the fire last night. And in a bizarre way, she had reinstated herself among the living too.

One night, one lapse of sanity might be acceptable. She

could still make a decision on this contract with a clear head. If it never happened again. If she wiped it from her brain…

The irony of it all made her shake her head as the marina came into view, sleek, expensive sailboats bobbing in their moorings. The one man who did it for her was the one man she couldn't have.

Le Belle Bleu was no Paradis.

Located on the northern tip of St. Lucia, on a peninsula that boasted the island's best beaches, Matteo could see why it had once been described as "one of the most dramatic resorts in the Caribbean" by a famous luxury hotel magazine. "A mermaid's paradise…" Surrounded on three sides by water, each suite boasting a million-dollar ocean view with a private plunge pool that connected to the sea, its world-class restaurants weren't just set on the water, they were *in* the water with glass floors, walls and ceilings immersing patrons deep into the sea with the most incredibly colored tropical fish as dining partners. And then there was the spa which was undeniably impressive with its renowned organic sea treatments favored by the globe's elite.

As far as Matteo was concerned, that's where the travel brochure ended and reality began. Five minutes into their walk-through with the hotel's manager, Raymond Bernard, it had become clear the property's ten-million-dollar face-lift was more of a disaster than a fix. If the shoddy renovations didn't bring the kitchen falling down around Quinn's head, the questionable wiring would. There was no way this hotel was going to be ready for its opening in two weeks. And from the scowl on Quinn's face, she'd figured that out too.

He asked another pointed question of Raymond since Quinn seemed to be too busy fuming. No doubt wondering how she was going to host every VIP in the Caribbean in this mess in two weeks for the relaunch of a hotel that was considered a national treasure.

Raymond gave a completely inadequate answer to his question. Quinn rolled her eyes. She appeared to have exactly zero patience for the manager who was obviously struggling in his role and wasn't trying to hide it.

They followed Raymond through the glitzy, opulent lobby. His ill-advised swim this morning had managed to knock some sense into his brain. What he'd done last night had been the height of stupidity. There were no excuses for it. But what he could do now was make sure it never happened again. Give Quinn no reason to think what had happened between them should have any bearing on her decision. He was going to prove beyond a shadow of a doubt that De Campo was the right partner for Luxe. And Le Belle Bleu provided the perfect opportunity for him to do that. He'd been through restaurant construction with De Campo's properties. Knew what to look for. Quinn's ice cream and hamburger franchises were built on an identical blueprint that had nothing to do with this type of scale. Complexity. Right now, she looked as out of depth as he had been this morning in water way over his head, unidentifiable sea creatures lapping at his feet.

Raymond stopped in front of the new kitchens and started detailing their attributes with as much enthusiasm as a tortoise sunning himself on a rock. "So," he summed up in that all-the-time-in-the-world West Indies drawl of his. "Impressive, isn't it?"

Quinn stuck her hands on her hips. "Not at the moment, no," she said sharply. "But it will be."

Raymond paled. "I thought you would be pleased with what we've done."

"I'm not exactly sure which part of this disaster you're referring to," she responded curtly. "We'll deal with it later. Right now let's review the menus so we can discuss them over lunch. That's what Matteo and Daniel really need to see."

They sat on the poolside terrace while Le Belle Bleu's head chef took them through the new menus he'd designed. By the end of his presentation, Matteo was convinced the lineup showed such an abject lack of creativity it wasn't even appropriate for a three-star hotel, let alone Luxe.

"Where is the seafood?" Quinn asked, jamming a hand on the table as if to physically restrain herself. "St. Lucia is a Caribbean island. People expect seafood."

The chef pointed to the entrées. "There are two fish dishes here."

"Two out of twelve?"

"W-we thought it was sufficient…. We have an international clientele."

"Who don't eat appetizers?"

"Well, there is some crab in this one…"

Quinn dropped her head in her hands.

"Quinn?" Raymond's placid tone was filled with apprehension. "Any other comments?"

"Yes," she snapped. "But since it's way past time for lunch, let's do it over that."

She sliced a look at Matteo and Daniel. "Consider this a work in progress."

They ate by the sea. When Quinn attempted to sit on the other side of the table from him, Matteo deftly presented the chair beside him with a gallant flourish.

"The view is much better here."

"I thought," she stated evenly, "I would save it for you and Daniel since I'll have more of a chance to enjoy it than you will."

"Oh, no," Daniel said hastily, clearly recognizing he was running this race a few too many steps behind, "the lady should have the best view, always."

Matteo's lips twisted as Quinn sat down. "I'm not sure 'lady' is the best description for you today," he murmured in her ear as he pushed her chair in.

She gave him a glare that would have felled a lesser man. "You're not giving the man a chance to breathe," he counseled quietly, sitting down beside her. "I would have thought Warren taught you allies make better bedfellows."

Her shoulders dropped. "He won't last long enough to become an ally," she muttered icily.

Matteo's return glance was reproving. "You need to take a deep breath."

She did. Lord knew she did. But she didn't need to hear that coming from him right now. "Don't think," she said in a deadly quiet voice, pretending to point out a particularly good bread in the basket for the other's benefit, "that last night gives you the right to cross the line with me."

He took a piece of cornbread. "Oh, I wouldn't dream of it," he murmured. "But we do have to talk about it. Have a drink with me before dinner."

She stared mutinously at him. The last thing she wanted to do, given her mood, was talk about last night. But she was pretty sure it couldn't be avoided.

She nodded. "One drink."

Matteo was waiting for her in the cliffside bar when she arrived, seated at a table near the sheer drop to the sea. Cool and elegant in black pants and a lavender shirt that only a man with the highest degree of self-confidence would wear, he made drool pool in her mouth.

He stood and held out her chair. "I ordered you a glass of the Riesling."

Her favorite in the heat. His powers of observation were incomparable. As they had been this afternoon, noticing everything she had not. Like some superhero with X-ray vision.

"Thank you," she murmured, sliding into the leather seat. "We're due to meet the others in a half hour."

He lowered himself gracefully into the seat opposite her. "I'll get straight to the point then."

Her head throbbed anew, despite the two painkillers she'd ingested. "Last night was an aberration," she pronounced sharply. "A one-time thing. Never to be repeated. Can we leave it at that?"

"We should." His mouth flattened into a straight line. "It would be disastrous for both of us for this to go anywhere."

She let out a sigh of relief. So good they agreed on that.

"I wanted to say thank you, however."

His huskily issued words made her heart skip a beat. "For what?"

He raked a hand through his close-cropped hair, and lifted his gaze to hers. "I'm not sure what I would have done if you hadn't come to me last night. I was in a dark, dark place."

The vulnerable gleam in his eyes, the tense set of his big body made the urge to slide her hand over his monumental. But she kept it glued to the table because this could not go there. It couldn't.

She swallowed hard. "I needed to exorcise my own demons."

"He's a jackass, Quinn." His harshly issued words caught her off guard. "I don't know what your husband did to you. I don't know what he said to make you feel like any less of the woman you are. But a man who would walk away from the woman I held in my arms last night is crazy."

Her heart went into free fall. "It's complicated."

"It's a travesty."

They sat there in silence because to say any more

would be going to a place neither of them could venture. Matteo took a long pull of his beer, set it down and gave her a steady look. "Le Belle Bleu will never pass its inspection, Quinn. You have a seriously big problem on your hands."

She exhaled deeply. "I know. But I'm not sure what to do. Raymond swears he has the best contractor on the island."

"And today convinced you of that?"

What alternatives were there? Warren had asked her to handle it, but she was no construction expert. And she didn't know the local business climate.

Matteo reached into his pants pocket, pulled out a business card and slid it across the table to her. "We've used this company to build some of our American restaurants. They have an impeccable track record and a presence here. I made a phone call this afternoon to them and they're willing to come take a look."

"In the next hundred years?" She pressed her hands to her temples. "I have an opening in two weeks. We need to at least have the kitchen in some sort of safe, working order. The rest we can do in phases."

"If they agree to take on the job, they would do the urgent items right away. *If* they agree to take it on," he underscored. "Because of De Campo's relationship with them, I think we have some leverage. They've offered to come look at the hotel next week."

"Really?"

He nodded. "If you like, I will stay and do the walkthrough with you."

Her lips formed the words *yes, please*. She needed his contact because no one else was calling her back. She was terrified Le Belle Bleu wasn't going to open on time. But she was also clear on why Matteo was doing this.

The closer he inserted himself into Luxe's operations, the harder it would be for her not to choose De Campo.

It was also so not her style to accept help and Lord knew, the Quinn of last night was a terrifying, alien creature not helped by Matteo's continued presence on this island. However, the panic raking its way up her throat was all-consuming. The hotel was a disaster.

"They will not screw you over, Quinn." Matteo gave her an even look. "I know these guys. If anyone can fix this, they can."

"All right." She nodded. "But you need to understand, this will in no way help you in the bid process."

He nodded and stood abruptly, his expression hardening into one that was all business. "Let me see if I can get them before dinner."

Matteo strode off in the direction of his suite. Quinn wondered why her heart was now somewhere in the vicinity of her toes.

He was going to help her, wasn't he? Help her drag Le Belle Bleu out of the mess it was in before her hotel chain's reputation went into the toilet? This was no time to pine for him to acknowledge how amazing their night together had been.

Her grip around her wineglass tightened. *Oh, my God.* That's exactly what she'd wanted him to do. She'd been expecting him to rehash last night, when all he'd wanted to do was help her relaunch her hotel, and, in doing so, ingratiate himself even more to Davis Investments.

Where in all this had she become *that* creature?

And if a man was crazy to walk away from her, then how had he just done it so easily?

Quinn, the queen of business, the queen of logic, suddenly had to swallow a very bitter pill. Last night might have been explosive. A once-in-a-lifetime chemistry. But she wasn't worth a ten-million-dollar deal.

It was that simple.

She stood up with a squeal of her chair that made the couple at the next table stare. It's not as if she should be surprised. When it came to Quinn Davis, there was always a reason to leave.

CHAPTER EIGHT

THINGS ALWAYS GOT worse before they got better.

Wasn't that the saying?

Matteo sat at the lobby bar of Le Belle Bleu knocking back a local beer as the last of the contractors beat a hasty retreat before Quinn could catch them and ask for just one more thing to be done. They were wary of her perfectionism, working like dogs to get the last cosmetic fixes done to the restaurant and bar before the hotel was unveiled to everyone who mattered in five days. But at some point they had to sleep. Not that Quinn seemed to have noticed. Or needed to herself…

When the scale of the work to be done had become clear, he'd offered to stay and help manage the contractors. Quinn couldn't do it all on her own and his familiarity with the contractors went a long way. He had to be back in New York right after the reopening for a board meeting and then in Chicago for the pitch, but at least he could help her get the doors open. Make the hotel shine for its debut.

He'd worked side by side, day and night with her and François to get the menus fixed and the human machinery of the bar and restaurant functioning as a five-star hotel should. Now it was just a question of execution. Could the chefs perfect the dishes? Could the bartenders master the complex cocktail list they'd created? Could the staff come together like the well-oiled machine they needed to be to impress a crowd that would be discerning to a fault?

He reached up and massaged the back of his neck. He was beat. Exhausted. But it was worth it. Daniel Williams had boarded a flight back to the outback looking utterly disgruntled at leaving the competition behind. Quinn was relying more on Matteo every day. It was exactly where he wanted to be. But funnily enough, this hadn't been all about his endgame. Quinn was struggling. She'd taken on a task no human being could do by themselves and refused to admit she was in over her head. She'd plowed ahead against the odds with a mind so patently brilliant he could see why she'd gotten where she had at such a young age.

They might, just might, pull this off.

His mouth quirked. Her management style could use an overhaul. Her passion for what she did meant she came on a bit strong. But everyone, right down to the busboys and bartenders, respected her work ethic. Even Raymond Bernard, presently making his way across the lobby with Quinn, seemed to be catching the fever. He might even keep his job at this rate.

The pair pulled to a halt in front of him. Matteo studied the dark circles under Quinn's eyes. She needed help. More than he could give her. She looked longingly at his beer. "Our sommelier's flight was canceled. He'll be here first thing in the morning instead."

"So we come back then?"

"We have a big storm rolling in." Raymond gestured toward the darkening sky. "I don't advise you driving back to Paradis under those conditions, not on these roads."

Quinn gave the sky an uncertain look. "It won't be that bad, do you think?"

The manager lifted his shoulders. "It's going to be a proper tropical storm. I wouldn't chance it."

Her brow furrowed. "Are they finished with the floors on any of the suites?"

"The Dolphin Suite, yes. I had them finish it in case you wanted to stay."

"That's it?"

He nodded. "Everything else is still being polished. That one has three bedrooms in it though."

Quinn caught her lip between her teeth. Matteo could have saved them all the breath and suggested that, no, staying here in a suite with Quinn with the electricity that raged between them was a distinctly bad idea. However, even he, a lover of windy roads and tricky driving, didn't relish the thought of traversing the narrow, hair-raising St. Lucian highways in a tropical downpour.

Quinn glanced at him. "Okay if we stay?"

"Of course." He could make it through one night with a single wall between them. Couldn't he? He'd managed to get through an entire week without putting his hands on her. Had kept things straight as a board between them. *This* was definitely doable.

"All right then, thank you," Quinn accepted. "We'll stay."

They raided the hotel boutique for a change of clothes while Raymond got them a key. Quinn held up a tangerine-colored bikini. "I need a swim," she said with a grimace. "Get yourself some trunks."

He stared at the curtain of the changing room as it flapped shut behind her. Was she crazy? What planet was she on? Sharing a hotel suite was bad enough. Getting naked with her was insanity.

Not happening.

Except he was severely hot and tired. He needed to unwind from the pressure cooker that was Quinn, and a beer in the plunge pool or hot tub was an irresistible siren's call. Mouth tightening, he grabbed a pair of trunks, an extra shirt and a pair of khakis. He could swim while she was working. God knew she did it 24/7.

Showered and changed into casual pants and a polo shirt, Matteo emerged from his bedroom into the main living area of the luxury oceanfront suite destined to house heads of state and rock stars, to find Quinn pacing the space, phone pressed to her ear, her gait agitated, voice sharp.

Not something he needed to be present for, he decided, walking out onto the terrace. He took in the forbiddingly dark sky, its ominous gray-black clouds that seemed to hang suspended over the island. Raymond had been right. It was going to be a proper tropical storm, hard and heavy, any minute now. There was nothing like an island rainstorm to relieve the tension and humidity in the air, and right now they both needed it. Badly.

He fought the urge to strip down and dive into the ocean and stay there. No swimming allowed until Quinn, in that sapphire-blue dress of hers, which made the most of her voluptuous figure, was safely immersed in work and the sweats he now knew she preferred to do it in.

Focus. Get the job done, Matteo.

Quinn's voice floated out onto the terrace, hard, determined. "No, Warren, I do not need you to fly down here. It's coming together."

A pause. "You don't trust me."

Another pause. "I'm fine. Focus on the U.S. hotels. The reopening will go off without a hitch, I promise you."

If everything fell into place. He winced as he thought about how much there was still left to do in five short days.

The rest of the conversation was short, abrupt. The ping-pong back-and-forth of two intensely driven, strong wills ended in a defiant silence. It was a good five minutes before Quinn joined him on the terrace, her green eyes glimmering with frustration, full mouth drooping with fatigue.

"Where is the wine?"

He poured her a glass of the sparkling white chilling in the ice bucket. "When," he asked quietly, handing it to her, "are you going to admit you're human like the rest of us?"

The tigerlike fierceness he'd come to know so well sparked in her eyes. "It's not that," she growled, taking the glass from him. "He never fully trusts me with anything. He says he does, then he undercuts me. He has to put his stamp on everything. Point out where I'm lacking..."

Matteo shrugged. "It sounded to me like he was offering help."

Her mouth twisted. "He only offers it when he thinks you're about to screw up."

"Maybe you're looking at it the wrong way," he suggested. "The most successful people in the world don't do it on their own. They surround themselves with good people."

She lifted her chin as if she hadn't even heard him. "Once, just once, I'd like to do it on my own. Prove that I am not successful just because I am Warren's daughter, but because of my damned impressive abilities."

"I don't think anyone's doubting that."

"Yes, they do. All the time the other vice presidents take shots at me. I've heard them behind my back."

He took a sip of his wine. "So you're going to spend the rest of your career worrying about what everyone else thinks?"

She pointed her glass at him, antagonism darkening her eyes. "Do you know that after I made the top thirty under thirty list, Warren did not say a word of congratulations to me? Not a word. He said, and I quote, 'It's too bad you weren't the first woman on it.'"

Matteo blinked. "Perhaps it's not his thing to give compliments then, but I'm sure he was proud of you. He had to have been. That list is brutally hard to get on to."

"I wouldn't be so sure about that," Quinn came back bitterly. "Warren's standards are so high you can't be human. You have to be a machine."

"How's that going for you?" he asked softly. "You seem to be doing a pretty good impersonation of one and it's still not making you or him happy."

She squeezed her eyes shut. "I just need to do better."

"No, you don't." He took a step closer. "Dammit, Quinn, you need to believe in yourself. You are working miracles here but you need help."

"I just need to get through the next few weeks and I'll be fine."

He sighed. "There are too many issues with too many properties."

"I will manage."

"You will self-destruct."

She looked him dead in the eye. "I didn't ask for your commentary."

He hissed in a breath. She could be a cold bitch sometimes. He'd been busting his butt for a week trying to help her and this was what he got? But even as he thought it, he knew better. Knew the puzzle that was Quinn had grown a hard shell to protect herself from getting hurt.

Let it go, Matteo. The voice of sanity echoed in his head. *Drop it now before you get more emotionally involved with a woman who is mortally off-limits to you.*

They ate at the candlelit table for two that overlooked the ocean, protected by a canopy as a crackling thunderstorm descended. It lit up the night with outrageously beautiful white light that arced across the sky and stole their breath. The small talk made him crazy. The need to hold her made his hands curl at his sides. He gritted his teeth and went through the key points to review with the sommelier in the morning. Forced the salmon down his throat. Did not acknowledge how she bit her lip against the electricity that raged between them every time their gazes collided, just as strong as the storm around them.

One more taste of her, he knew, and he was a dead man.

Matteo did not do relationships with women. Didn't even know if he was capable of one with his checkered past. With his parents' business merger as his prime example of what one could encompass. Quinn needed someone she could believe in. Someone who could restore her faith in men. Not him.

She offered him a liqueur after dinner. Coffee. He turned them both down flat. Watched the disappointment slacken her lower lip. "I have work to do," he murmured, getting to his feet and throwing his napkin on the table. "Thank you for dinner."

Then he escaped to his room.

Quinn poured herself another glass of wine and paced. She was out of control with her stress, no doubt about it. Matteo did not deserve her ire, not when he'd just spent the entire week bailing her behind out of an impossible situation they might actually pull off if they were very, very lucky.

It's just that he was so damn perfect sometimes. So calm and in control and able to see the big picture. Her fingers curled around her wineglass, absorbing its icy chill. That was, when he wasn't falling apart over a death he wouldn't talk about....

She stopped in front of the incomparable view of the sparkling sea that stretched for miles in front of her. And admitted it. Wasn't the real problem what a good job he was doing ignoring her?

She wanted to kill him. How rational was that?

Quinn stalked inside and changed into the bikini she'd raided from the boutique. Who cared if the sides were cut so high you could see her butt? Or if the triangles of fabric on the top didn't do a great a job of covering her chest?

Matteo had damn well walked away from her again. Without a backward glance. Which was absolutely their deal. It was. She just didn't know how he could so completely turn off his feelings. Forget how unbelievable that night they'd shared had been. Because she'd tried. She'd really tried. And it wasn't working.

She went back outside and sat on the edge of the plunge pool. The storm had moved off, silvery moonlight slanting across the smooth surface of the water, reflecting her confusion back at her. One night was supposed to have been all it was, yet she felt changed somehow. Matteo's hands on her skin, his passion for her, had replaced the fear and inadequacy Julian had implanted in her with the alternate reality that she was beautiful and desirable. Worthy of being treasured.

It had shattered a perception of herself carved over a roller-coaster year of marriage. She wasn't home enough, Julian had said. She wasn't warm enough to the wives of his business associates. Which had degenerated into the fact she wasn't warm enough in general. She didn't treat him like the man of the house.

She downed another gulp of the wine with a jerky movement. Her inexperience in bed had been a major disappointment to Julian. But now that that night with Matteo had proven she wasn't a cold fish, now that she'd sampled her ability to feel, to want, she was struck by the disturbing thought that she would never experience it again. That no man would ever know her as instinctively as Matteo did. Had from day one.

She sank her toes into the water. Lifted them out and watched the droplets fall like big fat tears from her skin. Hot moisture gathered at the corners of her eyes. She didn't want to be that person anymore. The woman who had written off a part of herself as unrecoverable. Who had never believed herself capable of more. A lump formed in her throat, swift and hard. Julian had taken away her desire to feel. Matteo had given it back to her. But he was just a play-boy doing his thing. He would move on now, win this deal. Focus on what was important to him. And Quinn would be left with the empty shell of who she'd always been.

The tears slid silently down her cheeks, shocking and unbidden. She hadn't cried like this since Sile had died. When she had finally lost the fight she had so valiantly waged against the cancer that had been too strong even for her adopted mother, who had been the most courageous woman she'd known. Now it felt like a fissure had opened up inside her and exposed everything. Every part of her. Made it painful to breathe.

The silvery moon dipped behind the clouds. Everything became blindingly clear in that moment. So blindingly clear that she didn't care anymore. She wanted more. She wanted her life to be more. The problem was, she thought, swiping the tears away from her cheeks with the back of her hand, she didn't know any other way to be. This was all she'd ever been. Quinn, who got the job done.

She blinked hard as the tears flew faster down her face. Matteo was damn right she didn't want to be human. Being human sucked.

Sometime around midnight Matteo, hot and unable to sleep, emerged from his bedroom and headed for the pool. The rhythmical song of the tree frogs filled the otherwise silent air with a deafening symphony he was surprised anyone could sleep through, yet he had slept through it these past couple of weeks, finding it exceptionally sooth-ing white noise.

But not tonight. He'd emptied his email in-box, read every last report and talked to Gabe who was presently wildly excited over a new wine. And he was still wide-awake with no sign his head wanted to join his body in its state of complete exhaustion.

He grabbed a towel from the rack and turned toward the pool. Then he froze as he saw Quinn sitting with her legs dangling in the water. Her gaze was fixed on the dark mass of the Caribbean Sea, her profile so exquisitely drawn he couldn't tear his eyes from it. He had never met a woman whose beauty was so all-encompassing—so layered. Just when you thought you'd reached the end of it, she revealed more of herself that made you fall deeper under her spell.

If he had continued on with his sensible behavior of late, he would have turned on his heel and gone back inside. Instead he focused on the spare amount of material in the tangerine-colored bikini that did little to cover her mouthwatering curves. Her upswept ponytail revealed the long, graceful curve of her neck that he wanted to sink his teeth into. Dammit. He should never have shared this space with her.

She sensed his presence as if a whisper of air had carried him to her. Looked up at him, the bright glimmer in her eyes wrapping itself around his heart and tugging. She'd been crying. Quinn, who took everything on the chin like a prizefighter and just kept on going, had finally showed a chink in her armor.

Run, a voice inside him warned. *Run before this all comes falling down around you.* Except he didn't. He stepped closer, lowered himself down beside her and dunked his feet in the bathtub-warm water.

"Couldn't sleep?"

She shook her head.

"What's wrong?"

She pressed her lips together. "I don't know."

He pushed a wayward chunk of her hair behind her ear so he could see her face. "You're too hard on yourself. You need to back off and accept help before you break."

"It's not that."

Just as Quinn had crossed the threshold into his room that night, Matteo knew what he was about to ask was the verbal equivalent of doing the same. But the words tumbled out of his mouth anyway. "Then tell me what it is."

She looked down at her hands. Twisted them together in her lap. "You made me feel alive the night we were together. Like for the first time in my life I could feel like everyone else. That I wasn't a machine programmed to churn out profit numbers…"

His heart stalled. "You aren't unfeeling, Quinn. You just don't know how to express yourself."

"I'm scared to." She lifted her gaze to his. "Being like this," she said, waving a hand at herself, "is the only way I know how to be."

"You can do it," he growled. "I've watched you command a room of fifty workmen with your pinky, Quinn. A little self-honesty is not that hard."

"All right then." She turned to face him, amber fire burning in her eyes. "You want me to face my feelings? Speak my mind? You said a man would have to be crazy to walk away from me and yet you've had no problem doing that.… Actions speak louder than words, Matteo."

"You know why I walked away from you," he said harshly. "You know why we both walked away."

She balled her hands into fists. "And so now you move on. You go your merry way, chalk me up as another of Matteo De Campo's conquests while I—" She stared down at her fists. "I am…conflicted."

Matteo felt as if someone should read him his rights. Tell him anything he said could or would be used in a court of law against him. Except his particular court of law was a ten-million-dollar deal that had become his personal hell.

"You see?" She sliced a hand through the air at him. "It's easy for you. You probably have a dozen names in your smartphone you're just dying to call when you get home."

"That is ridiculous," he muttered. "We are negotiating a deal that will make the front page of *The Wall Street Journal,* Quinn. This is not about our hormones."

"I know that." She slammed her mouth shut, wrapped her arms around her chest and did an impression of a statue. Saliva pooled in his mouth at the sight of her plush flesh fighting for freedom over her bikini top. God, he wanted to touch her.

Her eyes grew brighter, the delicate muscles of her throat convulsing. "Tell me what's really bothering you," he said roughly. "Despite what women think, we men are actually not mind readers."

"I'm afraid," she threw at him, aggravation lacing her tone. "I am scared that I'm never going to feel what I felt for you the other night for anyone else. That what we had was some one-night aberration and I'm going to go back to being cold old Quinn who can't have an orgasm because she can't let go long enough to let it happen."

His heart plummeted to somewhere beneath the concrete. "That's crazy. Of course you will."

She shook her head, lips trembling. "I'm scared I'm never going to feel that alive again, Matteo. It terrifies me."

"You will," he said hoarsely. "You just need to find the right man."

"The right man?" She looked at him as if he had cotton batting for a brain. "Am I the only one who thought what we shared the other night was inordinately special? Please tell me I'm not that big a fool."

He pressed his lips shut.

"Goddamn you, Matteo." She planted her hands on the ground to roll to her feet. "You could at least tell me the truth."

His hand clamped around her wrist. "You want the

truth?" She gasped as he yanked her back down, her thighs landing hard on his, her hand against his chest to steady herself. Blood pumped through his veins, filled his head with such pressure he was blinded to common sense. His gaze locked on hers like a heat-seeking missile. "The truth is I've spent the last week trying desperately not to make a mistake that will damn both of us. And if you think," he ground out harshly, "that there has been one minute I haven't thought about us together, then you can think again."

Her eyes were big pools of forest-green laced with gold, her breath unsteady as her fingers bit into his hot, tense flesh. A trickle of sweat made its way down his nape. "You were not a placeholder that night, Quinn. You were the only woman who could have saved me from myself. The only woman I wanted so blindingly much I could have lost myself on that night of all nights."

The hitch in her breath was deafeningly loud in his ear. He ran his thumb across the flushed skin of her cheek. "You know this would be a total disaster."

She arched into his touch like a feline craving his possession. "I don't care. I'm done caring. I will recuse myself from the committee. But if I'm just a deal to you, Matteo, you should walk now."

His heart pounded like an out-of-control freight train. "Quinn—"

She pressed her lips to his forehead. Kept them there. "I need to be with you tonight. I need to know I'm capable of more."

Perspiration slid down his chest, rivulets that pooled at the waistband of his trunks. He flexed his fingers against her soft skin, struggling for control. But this was bigger than both of them, this need for each other. It operated on a whole other level from anything he'd experienced before.

His hands came up to frame her face as he dragged his

mouth up to hers. "If we're doing this, if we're jumping, it has to be all-embracing, Quinn. I'll make love to you, but I won't have sex with you."

"What's the difference?" she whispered against his lips.

"Try it and find out."

His hands absorbed her still-damp, silky-soft skin. His mouth found the sweetness of hers, claiming it in a long, slow kiss that telegraphed just how this would be. She tasted like honey, like something he never wanted to leave. And he decided in that moment, if he was going to hell, he was going to enjoy every single minute of it.

"Matteo..." She breathed the word into his mouth, the edge of anticipation to it setting his blood on fire. His fingers sought out the knot of her bikini top at the nape of her neck and pulled it free, her soft ripe curves spilling into his palms. Her sigh of pleasure was like the most heady of aphrodisiacs. He pulled back so he could see her, drink in the rose-tipped perfection of her breasts.

"You knew this bikini was going to send me over the edge."

"Maybe."

He smiled, dipped his head and brought her nipples to firm, pink erectness with insistent sweeps of his thumbs and tongue. He waited until she was fully aroused and moaning softly for him before he slid his hand down over her stomach and eased his fingers under the elastic of her bikini bottoms. She was hot, wet and felt like velvet. Responsive to his every stroke. He wanted to taste her again, feast on her as he had before, but he wanted to sink his hard, aching flesh inside her more. To make her writhe beneath him until she begged for him to get her off.

He would. Eventually...

She arched under his hand as he stroked a finger into her. Took it deep. "God, that feels so good."

"I can make it better," he promised. He added another

finger, curved them against her in an insistent caress he knew would take her higher. She moaned and ground her hips against his hand. He smiled with satisfaction and brought his mouth to her ear. "This time we're taking it to the bedroom, Quinn."

She stiffened against him. "I said no bedrooms."

"Then you don't get any more." He pulled out of her, held her away from him so he could see her face. He struggled to control the beast inside of him that wanted to find Julian Edwards and extinguish him. "I don't know what he did to you, Quinn. What he did to make you so frightened. But I promise you, I will never hurt you."

He watched her waver. Saw the uncertainty flicker in her eyes. He rested his forehead against hers. "You have to trust me."

A tremor went through her. Her hands curled into his shoulders as if she were waging a war with herself. Then she burrowed into him. "Yes."

Matteo scooped her up off the concrete. Carried her across the terrace inside to his bedroom. When he set her down on the tile, he could feel the tension in her hips. See it etched in excruciating detail across the delicate lines of her face. He raked her hair back and let it fall down her spine, tangling his fingers in the smooth, satiny richness of it. "You say stop, I stop. No questions asked."

She lifted her chin. Put her palm to his pounding heart as if to steady herself, to feel the connection between them. He lowered his head and kissed her. Took her lush mouth again and again until she swayed against him, her hands circling his waist. "You make me crazy," he murmured, nipping at her lower lip until she bit back, sending his pulse into overdrive as her sharp little teeth sank into his sensitive flesh. "If you knew how many X-rated dreams I've had about that performance of yours on your knees... It was the hottest experience of my life, bar none."

Quinn pressed her lips against the throbbing pulse at the base of his neck. Dropped her hand to slide her palm against the rigid hardness of him. He went willingly to his knees. Slid his fingers under the almost nonexistent sides of her bikini bottoms and yanked them off. The musky, aroused scent of her hit him like a brick to the head.

"God, Quinn."

He put his mouth to her, drank in her essence until he was so crazy with want he thought he might lose it. Palms pressed against her buttocks, he held her to him, dragged his tongue across her, inside her. Made her cry out and dig her hands into his hair. She murmured unintelligible things, begged him to slide his fingers deeper into her in a caress he now knew made her crazy.

"Dammit, Matteo—"

He lifted his mouth from her. Pushed to his feet and brought her hands to the waistband of his trunks. "Take them off," he growled.

She shoved her fingers into them and ran them down his long legs. When she straightened and came back to him her face was pinched, expectant. He lowered his mouth to hers, sucked her bottom lip into his and kissed her until she was pliant beneath his hands. "Relax, *bella*. You say stop, we stop."

She rested her forehead against his and nodded. He picked her up and set her down on the massive king-size bed, her dark hair fanning out against the white silk sheets. She was creamy-skinned perfection, had the most exquisite hourglass figure he'd ever seen. Somehow he had the presence of mind to rummage up a condom and slide it on before he returned to her and smoothed his hand down over the curve of her hip, between the juncture of her thighs. Where he wanted to be.

Her eyes went huge. He straddled her, holding her gaze

the entire time. "Touch me," he rasped. "I need your hands on me."

She leaned forward and curved her fingers around the heated, throbbing length of him. He was sure he'd never been this hard, this aroused in his life. She was just that beautiful to him.

Her lips parted, the focus she devoted to his pulsing erection just about doing him in. He reached down, cupped her buttock in his hand and brought her thigh around his waist. "Take me inside of you," he urged. "I need to be inside of you so badly, Quinn."

She closed her fingers around him and guided him to her slick, hot flesh with that same intense concentration. He sank his palms into the mattress on either side of her and forced himself to wait. "More?"

"Yes."

He sank into her just enough to find his place. She arched her hips against him. "Please—"

He gave it to her, excruciatingly slowly, an inch at a time, waiting for her body to adjust to his. Waiting for her to relax—fully trust him. Deeper and deeper she took him, flexing beneath him until he was buried to the hilt. The shocked, dazed pleasure in her eyes had him whispering mindless pleas in Italian for control. He had never felt anything so good in his life as she clenched her tight muscles around him.

He let out a husky groan. If this was hell, he never wanted it to end.

Quinn wrapped her leg tighter around him, brought him closer. "Tell me," he said softly. "Tell me what you want."

She lifted her hips. "More."

He shook his head. "No. Tell me. I want to know what you like. What you need."

She began with soft, breathy requests that were half shy, half eager. He gave it to her, easy, leisurely, leashing the hard demand of his body to give her the buildup she needed. She caught her lip between her teeth. Her cheeks turned rosy. He urged her on with husky commands, goading her, making her tell him more. Making himself half-crazy in the process. Her demands became more insistent, more graphic. He hooked her leg higher around his waist and stroked even deeper inside her.

Deeper, harder until he was shaking with the effort it took to hold back. She flung a hard, raw demand at him that was the end of him. He swore under his breath and set his thumb to her center.

"Come, *sei bella,* Quinn," he murmured, dropping his mouth to hers. "Come for me."

She moaned and closed her eyes, pushed up harder against his thumb. Something inside her was still holding back, unable to let go. He held his screaming body in check and took her apart with one firm rotation of his thumb against her clitoris. Her hot contractions around him set him off like fireworks.

He kissed her, hungry, wild, his hoarse cry spilling into her mouth. And then there was only the long, sweet road back, his body cradled in hers, their connection so complete, so inviolate, he knew he'd never experienced anything like it.

Neither of them dared say anything. It was that heavy in the air. He rolled onto his side, took her with him, loath to break the bond. Her hot tears dampened his cheeks. He brushed them away, murmuring soft endearments in his native language until she fell asleep in his arms.

Moonlight poured into the room from the skylight, bathing them in an otherworldly glow. He stared up at it, his arms tucked securely around Quinn. He was definitely going to hell. He'd definitely passed Go. He'd definitely collected the girl.

It was a done deal.

CHAPTER NINE

QUINN WOKE WITH the birds, their boisterous song nudging her from a restless sleep that had seen her toss and turn most of the night. She wasn't used to sleeping with anyone. She and Julian had occupied separate beds for the last few months of their marriage when things had become intolerable, and Matteo's warm body wrapped around hers, his arm keeping her anchored securely against him was as alien as it was wonderful. She felt claustrophobic, secure and cherished all at the same time.

Light filtered through the skylight, sliding across the bronzed sinewy strength of Matteo's forearm. Her stomach did a slow roll, her fingers twisting in the whisper-soft silk sheets. Last night had been incredible...unforgettable. But had her need to be human been worth the fallout that was sure to follow? Because she had to recuse herself from the committee now. There was no other option.

Which meant telling her father she had developed a personal relationship with Matteo De Campo.

A wave of perspiration blanketed her skin. Throwing off the sheet, she slid her legs over the side of the bed and slipped quietly to the floor. Pulled on her bikini and padded out onto the patio where the first signs of dawn were tracing a hazy pattern across the sky. It was warm already but she knew the slightly feverish sensation heating her skin was the thought of disappointing her father yet again.

Watching the disapproval stain his blue-green eyes until she thought it would be easier just to turn around and take it all back. She pressed a hand to her stomach as her muscles tightened in a full-on revolt. Warren would not understand her letting her personal feelings get in the way of an assignment as big as this. He would be furious—questioning his decision to give it to her.

Standing there, watching the waves roll into shore, the surf rougher this morning after last night's storm, remembering how slowly, how exquisitely Matteo had made love to her, using his body as an instrument of pleasure, not punishment as Julian had done, she knew she had the answer to her question. She would do it a million times over. She felt as if she had truly honored her feelings for the first time in her life.

Quinn raked her hair away from her face with an unsteady movement. It wasn't as if she was ignoring the fact that she'd just made the career-limiting move of all career-limiting moves. It's just that the emptiness wasn't enough anymore. She'd had enough of it for a lifetime.

More troublesome, really, was who she'd just shared her soul with. Matteo De Campo, whose attention span with a female lasted about as long as his perusal of the morning paper.

She squeezed her eyes shut and breathed in the fragrance of frangipani, gardenia and magnolia. Matteo had said he wouldn't have sex with her, he would only make love to her. But he didn't love her. He lusted after her. And therein lay the real foolishness of last night's actions.

If you were smart, you didn't wait until Matteo ended an affair with you. You got out first before you were burned. Made a timely exit so the memories were good and the heart was intact.

The humid blanket of air bore down on her. She looked

longingly at the clear, turquoise water. Maybe a swim would cool her overheated brain.

Matteo woke to an empty bed and an urge for a woman that would have been disconcerting if he hadn't been wondering where in God's name she was. Followed closely by the even more disturbing reality that he had well and truly crossed the line this time and there was no going back.

A throbbing pressure filled his head. Expanded in his skull until it drove him from the bed and onto the cool tile to look for Quinn. It was like déjà vu, her being gone like this again, except this time everything was different. This time he hadn't slept with Quinn Davis in a self-medicating, over-the-edge fashion. He had made a conscious decision to be with her. To honor his emotions for her which ran so deep into uncharted territory he didn't care to contemplate them at the moment.

He pulled on his boxers and strode out onto the terrace, but it, too, was empty. Where would she have gone at just after six in the morning? Was she coming down from the high of last night and realizing what she'd done?

He winced as his head throbbed. There were consequences for both of them. Extreme consequences. He was going to have to tell Riccardo what he'd done, and it wasn't going to be pretty. But he couldn't do it until Quinn told the board, he knew the lay of the land and he had all his ducks in order. His brother would not see it as the complex situation it was. He would see it as history repeating itself in the worst, most reckless fashion possible. Matteo playing with another multimillion-dollar deal that could make De Campo's decade.

His low groan split the air. His brother was going to lose his mind.

Matteo paced to the other end of the patio, looking out over the water. He was a different man than he'd been three years ago. He had been laser-focused on this deal, had laid all the groundwork in a brilliant, understated fashion that would win it for them. He had done his job. Differently than Riccardo would have done, but strategically, it was perfect. Riccardo would crucify him anyway. He didn't get him. Never had.

He lifted his gaze to the sun slipping up from the line of the horizon. It struck him he should be taking the advice he'd given Quinn. He needed to stop trying to live up to everyone's expectations of him and do what he knew was right. Being with Quinn had been right. He knew it in his bones. He needed to convince Riccardo to believe in him. That he would win this deal regardless. That he had always had his eye on the prize.

He was about to go back inside and shower when he saw a lithe figure slicing through the ocean toward their suite. Quinn. He sat down on the edge of the pool while she swam the last hundred meters. She hit the edge, reached up to grip the concrete and blinked the water out of her eyes as she looked up at him, wet dark hair floating behind her like a mermaid come to visit.

He cocked a brow. "You like 5:00 a.m. swims too?"

She reached back and squeezed the water out of her hair, a rueful smile curving her mouth. "Only when I've had earth-shatteringly good sex with a man I'm supposed to be doing business with and I'm trying to process. Other than that I'm usually an end-of-the-day, sneak-out-of-the-office-for-a-class kind of girl."

"Earth-shatteringly good," he repeated, liking the taste of that on his tongue. "That's when you're supposed to stay in bed for more of the same."

"Did you hear me say process?"

"Processing is overrated." He leaned down, took hold of her hands and hauled her up onto the concrete. "Regrets, Quinn?"

She settled herself down beside him, water dripping from her wickedly good curves. "I think," she said with a wry twist of her mouth, "I've processed that right out of me."

"Good." He captured her chin in his fingers and lowered his mouth to hers for a long, lingering kiss. Her lips were soft and salty, capable of endless exploration. There was something so right about being with Quinn that he couldn't see the wrong in it. Even when there were ten million reasons why he should.

Her breathing was choppy when the kiss ended. "Maybe," she said unsteadily, "you should convince me some more."

He set her away from him with reluctant hands. "Maybe you should talk to me about Julian first."

She blinked. "Julian?"

"I want to know."

Her emerald eyes clouded, her gaze falling away from his. "There isn't much to say. Our marriage was a disaster on all fronts. Julian married me because I was Warren's daughter. Because I was the ultimate networking opportunity. He didn't love me and he couldn't cope with the wife he got in return."

He frowned. "What do you mean, 'couldn't cope'?"

"He wanted a wife who'd rather host dinner parties than work. Someone who was content to stroke his ego 24/7."

"Did the man not know you at all? That isn't you, Quinn."

"He thought I'd want to give it all up at some point. That he should be enough."

"Did you love him?"

She hugged her knees to her chest. "I was infatuated with him. He was good-looking, successful, everything I should have wanted in a husband. The catch of the century if the prebilling was to be believed. But then I learned who he really was."

A man who had hurt her so badly she didn't want to go near a bedroom… He ground his teeth together. "So what happened? I know he hurt you and I know the fact that you took up Krav Maga isn't an accident."

She looked out over the sparkling water. "I was inexperienced sexually when I married him. I'd had a couple of relationships, none of them great. Julian didn't like that. The more I disappointed him as a wife, the more I disappointed him out of bed, the more frustrated he was with me in it. The more he wanted to punish me." She pushed her hair out of her face in a movement he now recognized as a nervous tick. "The more angry he got, the more I retreated. I couldn't seem to please him. In the end, I was afraid of him. It became Julian asserting his dominance over me in the only way he could."

His body went tight. "He assaulted you?"

She shook her head. "I never refused him. I thought that would just make things worse."

Flames licked at his skin. "So what would you call it then?"

She chewed on the corner of her lip. "Like I said, he was rough."

He closed his eyes. "Quinn, why didn't you leave him?"

"Because he was Warren's choice. Because I knew the dissolution of my marriage would be my father's biggest disappointment." Her mouth turned down. "And it was. I don't think he's ever forgiven me for it."

His face darkened. "Please tell me your father didn't know."

She turned a scathing glance on him. "How would I tell my father that? Daddy, the man you wanted me to marry has verbally abused me every day of our marriage…

has been borderline abusive. Cheated on me with other women…"

The heat flaming through Matteo threatened to fry his brain alive. "He was unfaithful to you?"

She nodded. "At the end. But honestly by then I would have begged him to use someone other than me."

He pressed his fists against the concrete, the desire to use them on Julian Edwards immense. "You should have left. You should never have been with him, your father's choice or not. Warren would have lost his mind had he known what was going on."

"But you see that's not what we do." A haunted smile curved her lips. "We Davises specialize in making things work. No matter what. A merger, a marriage. You do not give up. You make it a success."

"That's an insane statement. What if he had escalated things? Started hitting you?"

She paled. "He wouldn't have done that. Control was his power. If he had that he was satisfied."

"You think that. That's how it starts, Quinn. It doesn't usually end that way."

She was silent for a moment. Lifted her gaze to the horizon. "He's gone now. That's all that matters."

He studied her defiant profile, her upturned delicate chin. "Didn't you ever think you deserved more?"

She shook her head. "I saw my marriage as my failure. I didn't want to admit I was incapable of a relationship."

"That marriage was not any kind of an assessment of you," he scowled. "Your husband was a monster. He should have been stopped."

She looked at him, the vulnerability shining in her beautiful eyes making his heart hurt. "I was hopeless at letting him in. I know in the beginning it was equally as much my fault as it was Julian's. I can be a supreme bitch when I want to be. I shut people out."

"Yes," he agreed. "But you can also be an insightful, compassionate, sexy, warm woman if you dig deep enough to find out." He ran a finger down her cheek. "And you aren't pushing me away right now."

Her gaze softened. "You," she said wryly, "are another matter entirely."

"Si," he agreed, reaching for her. "Story of my life, *bella*. But I know you like it, in fact, I know you *love* it."

Quinn was attempting to choke out a reply when he sank his hands into her waist, deposited her in his lap and pulled her wet limbs around him. "Sometimes the penny doesn't drop," he murmured, tipping her heart-shaped face up to his. "Sometimes things are exactly as you see them."

He watched that overactive mind of hers try and process that. Then she reached up and ran her finger over his bottom lip, a sultry glitter in her eyes. "What am I supposed to be seeing right now then?"

Matteo captured her finger in his mouth. Ran his tongue over the soft underside of it. Watched her pupils dilate. "You. On top of me. Now."

A dull rosy glow stained her cheeks. He released her finger. Bent his mouth to her ear, a raspy edge to his voice. "Up on your knees, *cara*."

She did it. Set her knees down on the concrete on either side of him. And he knew from the sparks in her eyes she was just as turned on as him. Needed more as much as he did.

He ran his hand down her trembling stomach, inside her briefs and explored her soft, yielding flesh with teasing strokes that made her body moisten and ready for him. He hardened so quickly he had to bite back a groan. Then she pressed her lips to his stubble-covered jaw, her breathing jagged, uneven, and he did it anyway. She was so sexy when she let herself go.

"Condom," he croaked, stumbling inside in an Olympicworthy performance. When he returned, she straddled him, released him and slid the condom on. He reached down and pulled her bathing suit aside. *"Portami dentro di te tesoro,"* he murmured. "Take me inside of you, sweetheart."

She reached down and grasped the thick, highly aroused length of him. This time his groan split the air in a fractured moan. Quinn brushed him against her core. Teased him. When he thought he might die, she took him inside her. Slowly, torturously, her gasp filling his ears. It made him feel proud, intensely male that he could do that to her and he swelled even larger inside her. Forced himself to stay completely still as she sank down on him. More, more, until he was buried completely in her.

She trembled in his arms. Dug her nails into his shoulders. He pushed her back, held her hair away from her face so he could see her. "You are the most beautiful, responsive woman I have ever had," he said huskily. "Never ever doubt your ability to feel, Quinn."

Her chin quivered, her fingers curling around his shoulders in a fierce grip that telegraphed her struggle. Then she brought her mouth to his and kissed him blindly. Soulfully. Until their union was taken to another level completely.

He dug his hands into her hips and lifted her. Brought her back down on him in a rhythm so slow and deliriously good he closed his eyes and savored it. The sound of them filled the air, the raw push and pull of their bodies heartstoppingly erotic. Quinn buried her head in his shoulder and whispered encouragement. Faster. Harder.

Her body tightened around him. Brought him torturously close to the boiling point. She begged him to make her come, needed his guidance. And he did, pulling her hips hard against him, placing a hand against her bottom and grinding them together. "Like that," he told her. "Use me."

She leaned forward and rubbed her flesh against him

with every stroke. His body tightened, ready to explode, and he cursed and told himself to hang on. Hold on for ten more seconds so that she could get there. Be with him.

Her soft cry shattered the air. She shook wildly beneath his hands as the orgasm tore through her and caused his. He arched his hips and let loose a guttural, primal grunt of satisfaction that might have traveled to Pluto it rocked him so furiously. They stayed like that, aftershocks ricocheting through their bodies, until he picked her up and carried her to the shower. Sensuously, reverently, he washed her beautiful body all over until he couldn't help but want her again and took her against the wall.

It occurred to him he might never stop wanting her.

CHAPTER TEN

ON THE LAST LEG of what seemed like an impossible journey to reopen Le Belle Bleu, things were finally falling into place. The night before the reopening, Quinn could almost see the light, although she wouldn't dare say it aloud for fear some other disastrous calamity might occur. But she was smiling for the first time in a week.

Optimistic enough that she had agreed to a stir-crazy Matteo's plan to take an hour's break to go for roti at the shack on the beach, legendary with the locals for its version of the piquant Caribbean specialty.

They both needed a break. Needed to let off some steam. A walk on the beach might do it. She pulled on shorts and a T-shirt in the bedroom she and Matteo were sharing in the suite at Le Belle Bleu in the hectic lead up to the relaunch, his clothes left in the other bedroom for optics, and pulled her hair into a ponytail as he showered. She hummed to herself while she slicked on some lip gloss, the glimmer of Matteo's sleek gold watch catching her eye on the dresser. She picked it up and tested the weight in her palm. It was an exquisite timepiece with diamonds marking the hours and an understatedly elegant black pearlescent background. A collector's edition, likely.

She turned it over to examine the back. Saw there was a finely drawn inscription laced across the matte gold surface. It was in Italian. And although she knew she shouldn't do it, that it was private to Matteo, she sat down and typed it into her computer to translate.

You meant everything to my son. Take him with you always. Affonso.

Her heart stuttered in her chest. The watch was Giancarlo's.

She replaced it on the dresser. Stood looking at it. Matteo's darkness had receded since that night at Paradis, but it still had him in its grip. She saw it in those unguarded moments, when his mask slipped and the haunted look returned. As if it never really went away.

She frowned. He called her a closed book. If she was a closed book, then he was a buried story. Pretending to be open to the world when he was anything but.

The sun was setting as they walked along the beach to the restaurant, if you could call the ten-foot-by-ten-foot brightly painted slatted wooden structure that. She kept the conversation light while they shared their rotis on the sand in front of the rolling waves, a cold beer beside each of them.

Matteo lifted his beer to his mouth and took a long swallow. "Have you heard from Warren yet?"

She shook her head. "I rarely hear from him while he's in Asia with the time difference. He may not get back to me until he returns to Chicago."

"He needs to know," Matteo said sharply.

"And he will." She slid him a sideways look. She didn't understand why he seemed so anxious about her telling Warren and the board about them. It was she who should be stressed. It was she that was severely curtailing her career with this decision. Her father and the board would ultimately make the right choice. The fair choice.

"He's back tomorrow regardless."

He nodded. Looked out at the ocean. "Have you talked to Thea today? How's the foot?"

Quinn grimaced. A fifteen-hundred-pound stallion had stepped on her sister's left foot yesterday while she was conducting an examination, shattering the bones in multiple places. "She's at home twiddling her thumbs, cursing that damn horse. You see," she pointed out, "I was right all along."

That won her a smile. "That was just bad luck."

Quinn pushed her roti aside and decided the only way to get him to talk might be to start talking herself. "I'm thinking while I'm making all these radical decisions I might like to get to know my sister in Mississippi."

"Have you had any contact with your birth family?"

"No." The hollow feeling that invaded her every time she thought about the parents who had given her away made her chest ache. "I don't really have anything to say to them. They chose not to keep me. They had another girl. End of story. But my sister—it wasn't her fault. I just feel like I should know her at some point. Even if we aren't ever close."

He lifted a brow. "You don't think there might be more to your parents' decision than that?"

She brought her beer to her lips and took a deliberate sip. "They gave me away and had my sister a couple of years later, Matteo. How else can you interpret it?"

He swiveled to face her. "Like maybe they weren't ready when they had you. Like maybe there are complexities involved you know nothing about. Life isn't black and white, Quinn, as much as you'd like to think it is. There are a lot of gray areas."

Gray areas. That's what you called giving your child up, never to see them again? Marking her defective in the process? "I wouldn't expect you to understand."

"Why don't you try?" he challenged. "There are no prizes for being an island, Quinn."

She turned to face him, latching on to the opening. "I don't know about that, Matteo, you are. You pretend to be everyone's man, but you're no one's man really."

His mouth flattened. "What's that supposed to mean?"

"Exactly what I said. You talk, but you don't really talk."

He sliced her an even look. "How about we finish with you before we move on to me? How is it you think I cannot understand what you're going through?"

"Because you have a family who loves you. Who are yours. Your flesh and blood. How could you possibly understand what it's like to not be wanted? To have Warren and Sile so desperate for a child they adopt me, then months later get everything they ever wanted in Thea? To not be good enough for my old family, and not be needed by my new one?" She blinked against the fire burning the back of her eyes. "It was heartbreaking, Matteo. Heartbreaking to grow up knowing that."

"And finally we get somewhere…" He pushed his dinner aside, sat back and wrapped his arms around his knees. "You know what I know, Quinn? I saw how much Thea adores you that night at the cocktail party. I heard how much your father respects you when he talked about you. Do you have any idea what I would do to have that same level of acceptance from my father? My family? I have spent my life fighting for it."

She pushed her beer into the sand, thrown again by another of Matteo's perspectives that upended her own. Was her frame of reference really so totally off when it came to her family? Was she so colored by the past it distorted all else?

"You live in a family of gladiators," she finally offered when the silence had stretched taut between them. "Isn't that what you do? Fight to be the best?"

He gave her a long, gray-eyed stare. "Perhaps."

She clasped her hands between her legs and looked over at him. "Giancarlo's father gave you his watch. Why?"

His shoulders stiffened. "I'm sorry," she murmured, "I was admiring how beautiful it was and I saw the inscription."

A shutter came down over his eyes. "There is nothing to be gained by talking about Giancarlo. He's gone. There's nothing I can do about it."

"Oh, for God's sake." She waved a hand at him. "You accuse me of being an island. You're so far out there you aren't even a speck in the ocean."

His eyes flashed with that lightning-storm intensity that signaled a clash of the elements was on its way. "I was responsible for his death, Quinn. I caused it. Is that what you want to hear me say? Giancarlo's father gave me that watch so I wouldn't feel guilty about what I did. Because he knew I would every day for the rest of my life."

Her mouth dropped open. "I'm sure that can't be true."

Matteo stared out at the horizon, his back ramrod straight. He was silent for so long she thought she'd pushed him too far. Then he dropped his hands between his knees. "Giancarlo was everything to me. My brothers, we're close, but I've never had the bond with them Giancarlo and I had. We grew up in Montalcino together, both of us groomed to be powerful men with the accompanying responsibility. Giancarlo became the CEO of one of Europe's largest car companies, a star of the corporate world, and I was running De Campo's European operations. We had power, money and youth. We were on top of the world. Drunk on our success…"

"Power can be an intoxicating thing."

He turned to look at her. "Giancarlo didn't handle it well. He drank too much, drove too fast, partied too hard. Maybe it was in his blood, I don't know. He had an alcoholic father with a high-flying job who managed to bury his issue under his success for years. It was not a good example. G told himself he could handle it, but he couldn't stop. Couldn't recognize his limits like the rest of us."

A chill settled over her. "Was he drinking the night of the accident?"

"Si." His hands curled into fists between his knees, a dark glitter entering his eyes. "I was annoyed with Riccardo for always handcuffing me, for holding me back from the things I wanted to do with the company. He didn't think I was ready and I knew that I was. So to spite him, to blow off some steam, I went on a tear with Giancarlo in Monte Carlo. We partied hard, won a lot of money, had more than a few women hanging off us willing to divest us of it. But at some point, my rational brain kicked in and I suggested we leave. G insisted we have one more drink to finish the night off..."

Her stomach rolled, pitched in a sickening twist. "That's why you reacted like that when Daniel pushed the drink on you."

His olive skin took on a white sheen. "Cognac was G's drink of choice...or perhaps I should say his weapon of choice." He shook his head. "I should have shut him down. I should have known it would put him over the edge. Instead I got caught up in the competitive thing we always had going on, had the drink and suggested a race back to our hotel."

"After drinking like that?" She couldn't keep the horror out of her voice.

He nodded jerkily. "I was out of control. *We* were out of control. We left—took different routes back to the hotel, and when I got there, G wasn't there." The blank expression on his face made her blood go cold. "I knew. I knew right away."

She put a hand to her mouth. "He'd crashed."

Matteo nodded. "I backtracked. He'd taken a one-way street the wrong way and wrapped his car around a tree. When I found him, the police were there, but there was nothing we could do to save him. He died in front of me while we waited for the ambulance."

Quinn's heart contracted. "Oh, God, Matteo—"

"He wasn't paying attention to any of the women that night." He went on, tonelessly. "He told me he was in love with his girlfriend, Zara. That he wanted to marry her and settle down and become a father because he knew this life we were leading was crazy. And he wanted better than what he'd had." His gaze moved to hers, a flash of agony darkening the emptiness. "A few weeks ago, I saw Zara's engagement announcement. That she's marrying someone else."

Quinn's throat swelled, thickened, until it was physically hard to get the words out. "You were both out of control, Matteo. You cannot blame yourself for what happened."

"I was the stronger one." He lifted his chin, the brief glimpse of pain she'd seen dissipating into cold, hard steel. "I should have known better. I could have saved him."

She took his jaw in her fingers, her eyes burning. "You can't save other people. We have to fight our own demons."

His jaw twitched under her fingers. "I should have done better. I *will* do better from now on. It will be my legacy to him."

A tear slid down her face. "You're a good man, Matteo. You have to believe that. I'm sure if Giancarlo could see you now, he would be so proud of you."

He was silent, the dying rays of the sun lighting the hard contours of his face. "Why should I get to be vibrant and enjoy the best years of my life when he is gone? I don't know if I can ever accept that."

She shifted closer to him, swung her leg over his, straddled him and brought his face to hers, the tears streaming down her face now. "Because somewhere up there he wants you to. Because the only tragedy worse than what's happened already would be for you to spend your life grieving for him instead of honoring him."

"But how?" he asked hoarsely, resting his forehead against hers. "How do I do it?"

"One day at a time," she murmured, absorbing the warmth of his skin. "My mother Sile once said it's not the mistakes we make that define us, it's what we choose to do with them. Choose your path, Matteo. Be better than your mistakes. And know, as G's father said, you were everything to him."

She sat there holding him, absorbing his pain, until his body seemed to give beneath her hands. Until she thought maybe, just maybe, what she'd said had gotten through to him.

They were silent as they walked back to the hotel, ankle deep in the sea, hand in hand. She had chosen her path, was starting to make pivotal decisions which would define her future. She just wished she knew they were right. Hoped they would carry her where she was going. Because she no longer knew where that was. She only knew she couldn't stand still any longer.

CHAPTER ELEVEN

IT WAS QUITE literally a miracle when Le Belle Bleu opened on August 5 with a VIP party that was next to flawless.

Italian marble shone in the opulent lobby, the cracks it had sustained during installation filled and polished to perfection. The connected series of fountains and pools which hadn't been close to finished when Quinn had arrived in St. Lucia were miraculously complete and bubbling with a magical shimmer that made them flow like liquid silver. And the hors d'oeuvres from the new menu being passed out by white-coated serving staff were spectacular—decadent and full of local flavor.

Quinn stood at the edge of the crowd on the torchlit patio by the sea as the evening shifted into the later hours and took it all in. She drew in a deep lungful of air and exhaled slowly, feeling her equilibrium right itself. It was the perfect debut for the legendary hotel. The blood, sweat and tears had all been worth it.

Bar staff moved seamlessly between the groups of guests who had decamped to the fire pits scattered around the patio. A reggae band played for the dancers. The shadowed profiles of every important personality in the Caribbean gleamed in the firelight, joined by their first round of guests and the global travel press. Her mouth curved. The staff hadn't missed a beat, polished to their own version of perfection by a newly inspired Raymond Bernard.

She might even keep him.

Lifting her glass to her lips, she took a long sip of champagne. Matteo had been right about giving Raymond a second chance. Right about a lot of things. He had brushed aside her mounting panic this past week and brought her back to earth, teaching her to take one day at a time. That with the right groundwork, everything would work out as it should.

Faith. It was all about faith, he'd told her. Not a trait she had a whole lot of experience with. But he'd inspired her to look deeper. To find it in herself. And in doing so, she had become a different person.

She sought him out in the crowd. He was talking to François and a government official, looking like the force of nature he was in a dark gray suit with an expensive sheen to it. The kind of handsome that made her heart race in her chest. Although she and Matteo had been unfailingly discreet during the day, given her inability to get hold of her father and recuse herself from the committee, every night they had come together in an insatiable melding of mind and body that had rocked her world.

It was crazy, dangerous, being with him like this but she couldn't seem to stop her headlong plunge back into the living. Being with Matteo was like ingesting high-octane fuel when she'd spent her life running on regular. And not even her promise to end it first was penetrating the rosy glow surrounding her.

He appeared at her side as if summoned by the pull of her thoughts, magnetic, lethal, far too disconcerting. "Stop looking for things to fix," he murmured. "The penny isn't dropping tonight, Quinn."

But it would eventually, wouldn't it?

"I can't thank you enough," she threw into the silence between them. "I couldn't have done this without you."

He lifted his broad shoulders. "We make a good team."

They did. He softened her hard edges. She made him tighten up on process when his creativity ran amuck. Their combined skills had made this night happen. One piece could not have existed without the other. And she couldn't help but wonder what it would be like to always have him by her side. To always have him.

Her lashes fluttered down. That was dangerous, silly thinking. Matteo De Campo did not do permanent. And neither did she.

He gave her a long look. "Dance with me."

She eyed him. "Not here, Matteo."

"A dance between business partners," he murmured, sliding an arm around her waist and ushering her through the crowd. She let him propel her through the guests, sure she wasn't a good enough actress for this. And when he took one hand and slid the other around her waist and started moving to the sensual rhythm of the reggae, she was sure she wasn't.

"I can't move my hips like that," she complained. "Can we do this later?"

He bent his head to her ear. "Let go, you little control freak. Let me lead."

She tried. Tried to match her undeniably stiff steps to his sinuous, smooth ones, but she kept stepping on his feet and stumbling to catch up. He wrapped his fingers tighter around hers and brought her closer to his body so he could force her steps into line with his. "It's a good thing there are times when you do know how to follow or a man wouldn't know what to do with you," he said roughly in her ear.

Heat filled her cheeks. "Matteo."

"What? No one can hear us."

She could hear her heart pounding in her chest, its insistent drumbeat reverberating in her ears. The burn of his thighs against hers was primal. The way he made her want to throw caution to the wind disconcerting in the extreme. She pulled in a breath and pushed back to put some distance between them. It wasn't just that he was the most charismatic man she'd ever met. He was also kind. Insightful.

She was a better person around him. Happy.

And tomorrow he would fly back to New York and she would fly back to Chicago and it would be over.

She stumbled. He tightened his hold on her waist and drew her back to him, those all-seeing eyes drilling into hers. "What's wrong?"

She was madly in love with him, that's what was wrong. Although she had no experience with the feeling, the inescapable, glaring truth hit her like a slap in the face.

She swallowed hard. "Nothing."

He studied her face. "Your lying skills have not improved."

"This has to end, Matteo. You know it and I know it."

His eyes deepened to that stormy hue that telegraphed a fight. "When did you happen to come to this conclusion?"

"You...I..." She shook her head. "We're flying back to the States tomorrow. To two separate cities. To two separate lives."

"So? This is the jet plane age, Quinn. Soon to have regular space travel."

Yes, but soon he wouldn't want her and she couldn't go through being left again.

He read her thoughts as effortlessly as he always did. "Oh, no, you don't," he growled, his hand tightening around hers. "We started this and we're seeing it through. I want you in my life, Quinn."

The crowd around them grew louder, buzzed in her ears. What did that mean, he wanted her in his life? For a month? Six? Until he lost interest and ended it, his contract intact? Until she went the way of all his other women, with a broken heart and a bar set so high no man could ever live up to it?

Her insides curled in on themselves. Julian hadn't even come home to pack his things. Instead he'd sent movers on a Saturday morning when she was still in her pajamas, barely awake and on her first coffee. She'd stared dumbfounded at them, wondering what they were doing there. Called Julian in Boston where he was supposed to be watching a ball game with his brother, only to discover he was with his lover of three months. And he was leaving Quinn.

The movers, he'd said, were the civilized way to end things.

After the movers had left, she'd closed the door, leaned against it, and slid to the floor. And hadn't been sure whether her tears were ones of relief or humiliation. Failure. All she'd been able to think of was what was she going to tell Warren. How she was going to explain his perfect match had been a failure before it had even begun.

"Quinn?" Matteo squeezed her arm, his gaze impatient. "Are you listening to me?"

She lifted her chin. "What's the longest you've ever been with a woman?"

His dark brows came together. "What does that have to do with us?"

"Answer the question."

"I was with my last girlfriend for six months. I cared for her, Quinn."

Six months. She, the failure at relationships and he, the man most likely never to commit were going to make this work?

"I think we should call it quits while we're ahead." She kept her gaze level, her tone even. "I'm about to put a major dent in my career aspirations when I tell my father about us. Perhaps that's enough for now?"

His gaze darkened. "Not when the only reason you're doing it is because you're afraid of failure."

Her blood fired in her veins, mixing with confusion to form a deadly cocktail. "What exactly are you offering, Matteo, beyond a hot affair with an Italian stud? What does having me in your life entail?"

His eyes flashed. "You had best take that back right now, Quinn."

Her gaze bounced away from his. "You know what I mean."

"Somehow I don't. Perhaps you'd like to explain."

"Your track record makes it very clear where this will end."

"This isn't about the past." A muscle jumped in his jaw, a heated fury building in his eyes as he captured her jaw in his fingers and forced her gaze back to his. "This is about the future. Our future. And you're trying to end this before it's even begun."

She pulled out of his grasp. "It's an act of self-preservation, Matteo. I have more brains than the rest."

His stormy gaze sliced over her. "You really are spoiling for a fight."

"That would be you, not me." She felt a set of eyes burn into them, fueled undoubtedly by Matteo's caveman tactics and turned her head to find the source. A photographer sat with a camera at the bar watching them intently.

"This is not the place to be having this conversation."

"You're right." He nodded tersely. "But you are not going to withdraw from me, Quinn. Get that through your head. It might have been an insane idea on both our parts to get involved, but it's done. Now, later, we are going to see this through. I promise you."

The music ended. She stepped out of his arms, relief flashing through her. "I should go talk to the governor general before he leaves."

His gaze followed her as she walked across the terrace with quick steps toward the governor. No way was she doing this now. No way was she making life-altering decisions when her head was clearly not on straight. Because agreeing to be with Matteo De Campo would have a ricochet effect on her life she couldn't contemplate right now.

It was the early hours of the morning before the party started to wind down and Matteo joined François at the bar for a drink, content in the knowledge that the evening had been an unqualified success. The tourism press and the VIPs had raved about the hotel's return to its former glory. The contractors would stay on to help Quinn finish the outstanding issues.

His work here was done. He and Quinn were not.

"Where's Quinn?" he asked François.

"She went to find a bottle of port for a guest. She said she'd join us after."

His mouth tightened. She'd been avoiding him ever since their conversation earlier. Deliberately. Unapologetically. He'd watched her shell come down around her as the minutes had ticked by. Shutting him out.

François handed him a shot of the ten-year-old rum he'd promised and babbled on about the night, his hands moving expressively through the air. Matteo lifted the glass to his lips.

This has to end. You know it and I know it.

Quinn's rash preemptive strike was festering like a gigantic sore. He didn't know it. In fact, he'd been avoiding the whole subject entirely until she'd said it. And as soon as she had, he'd realized he didn't want it to end. He wasn't ready to give her up. Might never be. But she was doubting what they had. Her history was kicking in and he didn't like it—not one bit.

Not when they'd both risked everything to be together.

He set his glass down with a thud. "I'll be right back."

Matteo's long strides carried him into the empty restaurant and down to the massive, ornate cellar. He found Quinn in the perfectly climate-controlled showpiece of a space, staring bemused at the rows of ports.

She looked up at him, hand on her hip. "Another request?"

"No. Which port are you looking for?"

She named it. He scanned the rows, yanked out a couple and found it. Setting it on the shelf, he caged her against the racks with his hands on either side of her.

"I'd like to know what's going on in your goddamned head."

Her eyes went round. "I thought we were going to talk about this later."

"Now. Why are you withdrawing? Why do I feel like we've regressed a week in a few hours?"

The delicate muscles of her throat convulsed. "Matteo, not now. I need to get someone a drink."

"And I need to know what's going on in your head."

She pressed a hand to her throat. Was silent for a good two or three seconds. "I'm panicking."

"About what?"

"I don't know, it's just all too much right now and I—I—"

"Spit it out, Quinn."

She glared at him like a cornered animal that wanted out, her emerald eyes sparking. "I am falling for you. I know it's stupid and I don't want to be but—"

He cut her off with a kiss. It might have been relief because it flooded through him like a life-infusing force. Or it might have been the need to put his mouth on hers and feel her sweet lips beneath his and know that it wasn't over between them. Because it couldn't be. She had wormed her way inside his heart, had become his weakness. And he couldn't resist her.

She sighed into his mouth as if she'd lost a battle and brought her hands up to frame his face. He wedged his knee in between hers and hauled her closer. Took the kiss deeper until he was sure he had branded her irrevocably his.

"You have to believe in us, Quinn," he murmured against her mouth. "This is real. We are real. And we are going to figure this out together."

"That's a nice cutline for the photo."

The amused voice came from behind them at the same time a bright light exploded. He jerked his hands from Quinn and spun around as another flash went off. *A photographer.*

The shorter, slighter man turned and ran. Matteo lunged for him but he was too quick. He fled up the stairs, Matteo in hot pursuit. Through the restaurant, out the doors to the terrace they ran. The photographer must have cased the place and knew exactly where he was headed, because Matteo lost him in the crowd. He stood there, breathing hard, his arms dropping by his sides. Damn.

He grabbed a security guard. The guard alerted his co-workers and they scoured the grounds. To no avail. The photographer was long gone.

Matteo sought out Raymond Bernard and demanded to see the press credentials. A white-faced Quinn joined him as the manager went off in search of them. She flicked him a glance. "I saw him watching us earlier while we danced."

"I don't understand." Matteo ran a hand over his head. "The door to the cellar locks automatically. You need a code to get down there."

"There's a ten-second delay before it locks again," Quinn said numbly. "If he was watching us and saw you go down he could have slipped in."

Matteo wanted to kick himself for being so indiscreet.

Like a cowboy with your gun drawn at all times, Riccardo had said. Was that what he was?

Well, he was paying for it now.

"It was a *Whispers and Tales* photographer," Raymond said, returning with a sheet of paper. He handed it to Matteo, a frown on his face. "Why would he be shooting in the cellar? It was not included in the permissions."

Quinn looked as if she wanted to throw up. Matteo studied the photographer's picture. It was definitely him.

He left a voice mail with Alex to put pressure on the magazine not to use the photograph. Threaten them with legal action. But it was 2:00 a.m. Chances were, the photograph would be making the rounds before she even had a chance to speak to his editor.

Quinn pressed her hands to her temples. "That's not going to make any difference, is it? They're going to use it."

"Probably."

They closed things off for the night, then headed back to the suite. It was nearly two-thirty in the morning by the time Quinn paced the floor of the living room, steam coming out of her ears. "With your notoriety, that photograph's going to be everywhere by tomorrow morning."

"Likely."

"We need a game plan."

"We've done what we can do for tonight." He kept his voice level, but his stomach was churning. The sense that he was on a one-way ticket to Hades binding its way around his brain. "It was a great night for Le Belle Bleu, Quinn. You did a superb job. Get some sleep and we'll figure the rest out tomorrow after I talk to Alex."

"I am not you." She went from agitated to Mount Vesuvius in under a second. "You might be used to having graphic photos strewn across the internet, but I am not."

He gritted his teeth. "I am generally very discreet about my relationships. This is not a usual occurrence for me."

"Yes, well, I have a reputation to protect. This is a disaster."

He took a step toward her, his blood heating at the gibe. "It's done. We can't take it back. There's no use being melodramatic."

"Melodramatic? You won't feel that way when my father hits the roof. When the board realizes how ethically wrong we've both been. Goddammit, Matteo. I was going to recuse myself. Now what is everyone going to think?"

"We will deal with it," he said firmly. "Together. It will be fine."

"You don't think Daniel Williams is going to see this and not cry bloody murder?" Her voice rose another octave. "I have breached an open bidding process with completely unethical behavior. It is not going to be fine. It's going to be awful."

"Quinn—"

She started pacing again. "Why couldn't you have just listened to me? Kept your hands to yourself until that party was over?"

"You want to discuss who hasn't been able to keep their hands to themselves?" He gave her a dangerous look. "Because you started this."

Color flared in her high cheekbones. She turned and walked to the open French doors and leaned against the frame, looking out at the sea. "It's not just about me, Matteo. De Campo could lose the contract over this."

He was well aware of that. Well aware of the nausea forcing its way up his throat, threatening to choke him.

"Panicking isn't going to help," he said grimly.

"My whole career is hanging in the balance." Quinn turned around, her face paler than he'd ever seen it. "What else would you suggest I do? I've spent the last seven years

killing myself to get where I am. To prove myself. People
are finally starting to respect me for who I am. And then
I do this. For *what?* For me to satisfy my need to *sleep
with you?*"

He went to her then, wrapped his fingers around her
upper arms and pulled her to him. "Do not start tearing
us apart because you're afraid. I told you I won't let you
do that."

"Why not? You haven't even said—"

"What?" He slid his fingers under her chin and brought
her gaze up to his.

"Nothing." She shook her head. "I don't even know
who I am anymore."

It hit him then. She wanted him to say he was falling
in love with her....

The words jammed in his throat. He cared about Quinn.
He really did. But he wasn't sure he even knew what love
was. How could he say it?

He might never be ready to say it.

He swallowed hard. "I care about you," he said gruffly.
"I told you earlier I want you in my life."

She looked up at him, her pupils dilating like those of
a wounded animal. "Really it was my fault wasn't it? Falling for a playboy? Because what does that really mean?
You want me in your life until you eventually tire of me?"

"Quinn—"

She held up a hand. "I've had enough for one night. Like
you say, let's see what the morning brings."

She marched toward the bedrooms. He watched her
go, chest tight, the injured look on her face almost making him go after her. But what would he say? He'd forced
her to open up and now he didn't know what to do with
the information he'd unearthed.

His mouth tightened. He jammed his hands in his pockets to restrain himself. It was a better idea to let them both

cool off and focus on the fact they'd just put a ten-million-dollar deal in jeopardy. His own career, his relationship with his family was hanging in the balance if he didn't figure a way out of this.

He needed an action plan and he needed it fast. Now was a time for logic. Not emotion. Because, undoubtedly, all hell was about to break loose.

CHAPTER TWELVE

IT WAS WORSE than he'd envisioned.

Matteo sat at his computer the next morning, a half-drunk cup of coffee by his side, the *Whispers and Tales* photo emblazoned across his screen. The placement of his hands made him wince. The cutline made him think selling wine to the devout might actually be a viable occupation.

He read it again to make sure it was as bad as he thought.

A Merger Made in Heaven?
After cutting a swath through the globe's most eligible women, all eyes have been on devastating Matteo De Campo to see which leading lady he'd end up with next. Seems the much-sought-after bachelor might have his sights set on a very lucrative merger between the De Campo and Davis clans. De Campo, seen here engaged in a passionate clinch with Luxe Hotels vice president, Quinn Davis, during the reopening of the chain's legendary property, Le Belle Bleu, in St. Lucia, seems to be having no trouble melting the heart (or other parts) of the "ice princess." We give this particular merger a hearty thumbs-up.

Damn. He sat back and pressed his palms to his temples. If he was Daniel Williams, he'd be out of his mind.

Questioning the integrity of all of it. The board, War-ren—who knew how they'd handle it? And then there was Riccardo. He'd wanted to have all the facts, know who the new decision-makers would be so he could assure his brother he had things under control.

Not happening now.

Quinn came out of her bedroom, dressed and bleary-eyed. "It's up," he said grimly. She sat down beside him and scanned the cutline. Her skin paled. His chest tight-ened. "Quinn—"

She stood up. "I need to head Warren off at the pass. My flight doesn't get in until eight. Can you take me in the jet and drop me off first?"

"Si." He stood up. "Do you want me to come with you?"

Her eyes flashed with an icy brilliance. "I run multimillion-dollar companies, Matteo. The last thing I need is to be babysat by you."

"I was offering to support you, not babysit you."

"I need neither, thank you." She headed toward the bed-room. "I'll be ready in thirty minutes."

He glanced at his watch. Heard a beep as a text came in. Riccardo.

Meet me at the house when you get in.

He sat down, a feeling of such intense déjà vu rolling over him it was hard to breathe. *"Mi deludi,"* Riccardo had said that night after the airline pitch. *You disappoint me.*

It had been the second-worst moment of his life. See-ing G's car wrapped around that tree the absolute lowest.

Alex called. Asked him point-blank if he was having an affair with Quinn. He confirmed it, wincing as she swore in his ear. "Do not say a word to anyone, not even the goddamned air hostess, Matteo," she warned him, and arranged to meet him at Riccardo and Lilly's to discuss damage control.

They did the flight up the East Coast in silence. When they landed at O'Hare, Matteo helped Quinn off the jet, his pilot anxious to keep their stop short and move on to New York. His mind trained on his upcoming confrontation with his brother, he gave her a quick, hard kiss. "I'll call you." Then he stepped back on the plane, the pilot went through his preflight takeoff checklist and they were back in the air.

He leaned his head back against the leather seat. His plan consisted of one strategy and one strategy only. He had to hope that Warren Davis was a reasonable man, that the board allowed De Campo to pitch and he won it so outright that no one would ever question his relationship with Quinn.

There was no backup plan. There was nowhere to hide. This was it.

Two and a half hours later, he stood on the back terrace of Riccardo and Lilly's Upper East Side Manhattan town house. His brother's jerky, barely controlled movements as he poured each of them a scotch sent Matteo's shoulders to his ears. "You need to let me explain," he started in a preemptive strike. "I care about her, Riccardo."

His brother whipped around, eyes blazing, a half-filled glass in his hand. "You care about her? I told you to keep your hands off her, Matty. Once, just once, I asked you to do something for the betterment of this company. And you're telling me, with all the women on this planet who would beg for you to *screw* them, you care about Quinn Davis so much you had to *do* her?"

Matteo took a step toward him. "Watch your mouth."

His brother slammed the glass on the bar, his legs

spread wide in a fighting stance. "Right now I'd like to take your head off, Matty. I swear to God…"

He swallowed hard. "I think I'm in love with her."

"I don't care if you think she's the future mother of your children. You cannot have her."

"Well, that's unfortunate," he said quietly. "Because I intend to."

Riccardo's ebony eyes bored into him. His nostrils flared, his fists balled tight by his sides. For a single, heart-stopping moment Matteo thought his brother would finally hit him. Let loose the aggression that had been pulsing between them for years. He stood his ground, his body tense with adrenaline. But it was like a crystal clear clarity had come over him. He *could* see Quinn as the mother of his children. For the first time in his life, he saw that potential with a woman. And he wasn't giving her up.

Riccardo let out an oath, picked up a glass and shoved it at him. Then he retrieved his own, filled it the rest of the way and took a long swig. "I have tried to be patient. I have tried to give you the benefit of the doubt time and time again, Matty, but I am very afraid you have inherited Giancarlo's death wish and I no longer know what to do with you."

Matteo felt the blood drain from his face. "I admit for the last couple of years I have been out of control. I had lost my way. But I am back. I have spent the last two weeks laying some brilliant groundwork to win this deal. Luxe will choose us."

"*If* Warren Davis does not eliminate us from the process after he finds out you have been screwing his daughter. *If* Daniel Williams doesn't make such a stink Luxe can't help but eliminate us."

His jaw hardened. "Quinn will not let that happen. She knows the right choice."

"She is compromised."

"She is going to recuse herself. And she will make her thoughts known. I know her."

"That doesn't mean the committee will go her way."

"I will convince them when I'm in that room."

Riccardo's lip curled. "Do you really think I should let you walk into that pitch given everything that's happened? If I were a smart man I would end this and do it myself."

Matteo's jaw tightened. "If you are a smart man you'll keep with the plan. I know the company. The players... I will win this."

His brother shook his head. "I must be mad."

"You need to trust me."

Riccardo paced to the other side of the terrace and stood looking out at the glasslike surface of the pool. When he turned back, his face was grim. "So help me God, Matty, it will not be just our business relationship that's in jeopardy if you let this family down."

A potent surge of anger raged through Matteo. He strode forward until he was toe-to-toe with his brother. "You always think I care less, Riccardo. That everyone cares less than you do. Well, you'd be surprised if you dug deep. Because I care. I care more than almost any damn person in this company." He pointed a finger at him. "I will win this for you, but on my own terms. Quinn Davis is nonnegotiable. Take it or leave it. That's my offer."

A long moment passed as Riccardo's hard gaze rested on his face.

"Do it then."

CHAPTER THIRTEEN

SUMMER IN CHICAGO got just about as hot as anywhere.

Quinn nudged the café door open with her hip, keeping her two iced coffees tucked to her chest as a wall of heat greeted her. The roiling, hundred-degree temperatures that had blanketed the city all weekend had stayed with them for the start of the workweek. She'd had a trickle of sweat rolling down her back not two minutes down the sidewalk.

She longed for the cooling breezes of the Caribbean. For the peace she'd found there.... Yes, they'd worked like dogs getting Le Belle Bleu up and running, but being with Matteo had made her feel settled in a way she'd never experienced before. They had been in their own private bubble, sheltered from the world. And maybe that was the problem. As soon as reality had hit, it had felt as if everything was falling apart.

She wound her way around a group of tourists, and headed for the gold facade of the Davis offices. The minute she'd taken one step into the O'Hare airport, Matteo's distant "I'll call you" ringing in her ears, the familiar anxiety had surfaced. The need to be someone she didn't want to be anymore. The uncertainty of who she wanted to be.

Then she'd faced off against her father. He'd been furious, as expected, questioning her commitment to the job with no regard for her personal feelings which had, in turn, prompted her anger and the devolution of their conversation into a whole lot of issues that had nothing to do with the deal. But she'd convinced him and the board to keep De Campo in the final two. Her father had appointed Walter Driscoll, Luxe's Chief Operating Officer, to take her place as the head of the committee, smoothed Daniel Williams's feathers, and her fall from grace had been cemented.

Now she could focus on doing her job. Except, she thought, lips compressing as she pushed her way through the revolving doors of the Davis building, everyone she worked with seemed to be reveling in the controversy, whispering behind her back. The tabloids had been having a field day, and worst of all, she missed Matteo like crazy.

She'd responded to his texts and calls to see if she was all right with polite if brief responses, as if her self-preservation was finally kicking in. Because if she'd had reservations before of things working out with a playboy like Matteo, the media coverage over the weekend had persuaded her she could never live in a fishbowl like this.

She exited the elevator on the executive floors, stopped at her PA's desk to drop off her coffee and pick up her messages, and shook her head as Kathryn held up a newspaper. "No more. I can't take it. Let it be a mystery to me."

"Perhaps you might prefer the life-size version lounging in your office," her PA purred.

Her heart jumped—raced in her chest like a jackhammer. She pressed the sheaf of papers against it. "Matteo is in my office?"

Kathryn nodded with a sly smile. "I didn't think he needed an appointment."

The prevailing attitude from everyone here all day. An intense, persistent interest in her personal life. Quinn the ice queen demystified as a human after all.

She stood there torn by how much she missed him and the desire to be her smart, rational self.

Kathryn flashed her an amused look. "Are you just going to leave him in there?"

She pursued her lips. "I'm trying to decide how the new Quinn would do this."

"I would start by closing the door," her PA said archly. "I like the new Quinn, by the way."

So did she. Although she was scary as hell and none too certain about the transformation.

Minimalist, fern-endowed and done in creamy, soft colors, her office was the perfect backdrop for a sensational-looking Matteo, draped across her desk, immersed in his smartphone. Dressed in dark pants and a light gray shirt with a contrasting darker charcoal tie, he looked like a cool, elegant drink of water.

She stopped inside the door and stuck her hands on her hips. "The pitch is not until Friday, you know."

He looked up and smiled that slow, easy grin that made her already excited heart go pitter-patter. "I'm here to see you."

She swallowed. "You trying to stir up more gossip and speculation parking yourself in my office like this?"

He gave her an even look. "I'd prefer to pursue the real story."

Which is?

"Shut the door, Quinn."

She stepped backward and pushed it closed, if only to prevent even more gossip.

He tilted his head to one side. "When you've taken my calls you've been annoyingly brief. Same with your texts. How am I supposed to know how you are if you won't talk?"

She shook her head, trying desperately not to fall into the trap that was Matteo because therein lay disaster. "Hasn't any of this craziness convinced you I was right in St. Lucia? This has to end?"

"Was *I* not clear enough we are going to work through this together?"

She sank her teeth into her bottom lip. Tucked the papers under her chin.

"Come here." He held out a hand and dammit if her feet didn't obey as if she was a trained animal. He smelled like spice and Matteo and when he tucked her between his legs and pushed her hair out of her face, it was the most right place on earth.

"First of all," he murmured, holding her gaze, "thank you again for ensuring De Campo's position in the pitch."

"It was the right thing to do."

"Secondly," he drawled, "I know you wanted me to say I was falling in love with you the night of the party. But I need to do things in my own time, Quinn. I have baggage too."

Her stomach did a loop-the-loop, ending up somewhere in the base of her abdomen. "I don't know how to play this game," she said huskily. "I need more, Matteo, to hang in here with you because right now this is all too much for me."

His eyes flashed. "What do you need me to say?"

She shook her head. She didn't even know.

"This isn't about the deal, Quinn," he said harshly. "I could pull De Campo out of it but it still wouldn't help with your trust issues."

"*Earned* trust issues."

He sighed. Lifted his hands to cradle her jaw, his smoky eyes holding hers. "I'm crazy about you, Quinn. I'm falling so hard it terrifies me. But this is a place I've never been before. You have to cut me some slack."

She felt her insides liquefy. "How are two commitment-phobes supposed to make this work?"

"Because it's you and me," he said softly. "And we are perfect together."

If anyone could have expected her to hold up after that, they were sadly mistaken. She rose on tiptoe, set her mouth to his and let her kiss show him how much she'd missed him. It was about two seconds before it burst into full-on flames. Matteo made a sound low in his throat and set her away from him. "If you want a decrease on the gossip you'd better cut back on that." He rubbed a hand across his jaw. "Please tell me you don't have plans for tonight."

"I do," she said with a nod. "With my bathtub. I could possibly amend it to include you."

The slow smile that stretched his lips pulled her insides tight. "I will make it worth your while, *cara*."

The new Quinn was fully in evidence as they left the office just after five. They stopped at a local grocery store, bought some cheese Matteo knew far more about than she did and a bottle of wine and took them back to her penthouse apartment in the Loop.

Far more than she needed with three bedrooms and an impossibly gorgeous view of the skyline, it had been an investment. Matteo walked to the edge of the lushly landscaped terrace and took in the view as she worked the cork out of the Pinot Noir he'd chosen.

"So how did your conversation with your father really go?"

She'd given Matteo the glossed over version of her no-holds-barred confrontation with Warren. "He thinks my judgment is way off." She poured the wine and walked over to hand him a glass. "He thinks you're using me to get the contract."

He winced. "Quinn—"

She held up a hand. "I know it's not true and I told him that. I also told him I needed him to be more of a father than mentor sometimes. That the tough love can be too much."

"And what did he say to that?"

Her mouth twisted in a wry smile. "I think he was flabbergasted. He thinks I'm as tough as him which clearly I am not." She shrugged. "He also pointed out I am not the best of communicators."

Matteo's face softened. "We'll call that an understatement."

"I also told him about Julian."

"Did he have any idea?"

"I think he didn't want to have any idea. He was horrified. But I think maybe it made him understand me a bit more. Understand why I've been the way I've been. Done the things I have."

He stepped forward, slid a hand behind her neck and pulled her into him. "You see? It wasn't that hard."

His heat, his strength enveloped her, swept over her like an elemental necessity of life she couldn't do without. She reached up and cupped his jaw in her hand. "I can't do another Julian, Matteo. If you leave now, nobody gets hurt."

He shook his head. "Getting hurt is part of life. But I am not going anywhere and neither are you. We are going to do this together. *Capisci?*"

Tears stung her eyes. "Yes."

He swept her up into his arms and carried her inside. She guided him to the master bedroom with soft, husky instructions. Peeled the clothes from his taut, muscular body with hands that shook with emotion. She wanted, needed him to possess her, to fill the void inside so badly it hurt.

He divested her of her clothes in a haphazard, completely un-Matteo-like fashion. His urgency should have frightened her, set off the old alarm bells. Instead she urged him on with husky commands. Told him how much she wanted him. Needed to know he could possess her completely, that she could give herself to him without reservation.

That she had the power of surrender.

He sensed it. Pushed her further. Set his hand to the small of her back and held her firmly against the mattress while his other hand slipped between her legs and brought her to hot, wet readiness.

"Matteo," she groaned, wild for him. "I need you."

The sound of foil ripping filled the air. He came back to her, slid a hand under her stomach, lifted her so he could bring the thick, insistent pressure of him against her pulsing core.

"You want me to take you," he rasped.

She gasped as he brushed the wide tip of his erection back and forth along her aching flesh. "Yes, now, please…"

He took her with a powerful thrust that stole the breath from her lungs. He was dominant, fully in control, using her body for his pleasure. His palm on her back held her secure, made her take all of him, but it was her pleasure, too. She felt him everywhere, stroking into her. Wildly excited, she pushed her hips up, meeting him stroke for stroke, murmuring her appreciation as he took her higher, gave her more.

When she couldn't take it, when she begged him in broken pleas to make her come, he flipped over on his back, his arm banded around her waist so she came with him. He was still buried deep inside her and brought his thumb to her clitoris. Maddeningly, insistently, he rotated against her pulsing flesh until she screamed, hurtling into the most intense orgasm he'd ever given her.

His big body pulsed inside of her, his hands clamped down on her flesh as he groaned and came. Made her his from the inside out.

They fell into a hot bath, had their wine and cheese on the bed. Then he wrapped her in his arms and held her. It was perfect, so perfect Quinn stayed awake long after Matteo's raspy snore sounded in her ear.

Maybe it was the lingering effect of always waiting for

the penny to drop—maybe it was because her father had pretty much said she and Matteo wouldn't last. But she couldn't help but wish he'd offered to walk away from the pitch. Had made his feelings for her that clear.

But he was right. She had to learn to deal with her trust issues. She needed to have faith in him. The problem was, she was still very, very new at this faith thing.

CHAPTER FOURTEEN

MATTEO WAS ADDING some last-minute statistics to his pitch presentation over coffee on Quinn's terrace when his mobile pealed, wrecking his concentration. He glanced at the screen. It was Gabriele.

"This better be good," he barked into the phone. "As you know my future with the De Campo family rests on me nailing this presentation tomorrow."

"No pressure there," his perfectly controlled, sanguine brother came back, rich amusement flavoring his tone. "Win and De Campo moves to another level entirely, lose and you are the permanent black sheep."

Matteo scowled. "You called for a reason?"

"I need you down here for a meeting today. I finally nailed an audience with the liquor board. The director had a last-minute cancellation."

Matteo pulled the phone away from his ear and stared at it. "You want me to fly to California *today* for a meeting?"

"A late afternoon meeting and dinner. You can head back first thing in the morning in plenty of time for the pitch in the afternoon. Rehearse on the jet."

He brought the phone back to his ear. "No way, *fratello*."

"I need you there, Matty. The director is a woman, apparently she knows you."

Matteo stood up and paced to the edge of the terrace. "I've stopped renting myself out as a stud, Gabe."

"Her name is Katlyn Jones. Remember her?"

Ah. He did. She'd been at a couple of parties he'd attended with his Hollywood ex.

"You're killing me, Gabe."

"Two years, Matty. Two years I've been waiting for this. To get them listening about the Malbecs."

"Two years I've been in purgatory, *fratello mio*."

"So we'll both win. Be here for two. I promise I'll get you back in time."

The line went dead. He dialed their pilot with a low curse, then his PA and went inside to change. Texted Quinn his whereabouts from the cab to the airport. And thought about the doubts he still saw in her eyes every time the contract came up. Since he was now sure he was fully, irrevocably in love with her, perhaps he needed to do something to demonstrate exactly how serious he was.

Quinn let herself in the penthouse, juggling an armful of groceries, her heart thumping in that ridiculous way it did any time she was about to see Matteo. She had taken the rather risky step of attempting to cook dinner for him given he'd been working until all hours getting ready for the pitch and as far as she could see, not eating very much. Risky when it happened she couldn't cook at all. But being with Matteo these past few weeks had inspired her to try a lot of new things. To push beyond who she'd thought she was.

She deposited the groceries on the counter and headed out to the terrace where Matteo preferred to work. They'd agreed he would stay with her until the pitch was over and take it from there. Figure out their schedules. But the door to the outdoor space was locked and there was no sign of him.

Figuring he'd gone for a run after the heat of the day, she slipped on an apron in the kitchen and started the water boiling. How hard could pasta be? Boil the water and put the pasta in. Throw it against the wall, apparently. But dicing? That was a foreign language. She took a wild guess and started chopping the vegetables into bite-size pieces. Thought how quiet, how lacking in life the apartment was without Matteo in it. How much she wanted him to come home so she could tell him about the insane step she'd taken of contacting the adoption agency to get in touch with her birth parents. Who knew where it was all going to end, but at least she might get some closure.

Butterflies swooped through her stomach. She shooed them determinedly away. Baby steps, that's how she was going to do this. With Matteo too. The scariest part was how easily she could see him fitting into her life. Last night he'd started talking about how he'd love a house in Lincoln Park, and it had not been a stretch to picture herself living there with him. Which wasn't baby steps at all. It was a huge, monstrous step that should have made her run, terrified. Except she hadn't.

She reached for the prosciutto rather than address the adrenaline surging through her. She loved him. She finally understood what it was that had been missing with Julian. How your heart could feel so empty with one person and so full with another. How when it was right, it was just right.

When the pasta sauce was done and "reducing" in the pan, she went into the bedroom to change. The clock on the bedside table read 8:00 p.m., which made her frown because surely Matteo should be back from a run by now? She reached for her Harvard sweats hanging over a chair. Noticed Matteo's overnight bag that had been lying in the corner was gone.

Her stomach seized. She strode into the bathroom. His toiletries were missing from the counter. She went into the living room and checked the table where he kept his laptop. Gone.

He was gone.

A buzzing sound filled her ears. Julian had walked out the door that day to Boston as if it was a run-of-the-mill trip to see his brother. And he'd never come back. Bile rose in the back of her throat. Had Matteo left her?

She gave her head a violent shake. That wasn't him. He wouldn't do that to her. She picked up her mobile and called him. Got his voice mail. Checked her email and texts to make sure she hadn't missed anything.

Nothing.

She thought about calling his PA but it was late and it didn't seem appropriate at this time of night, so she showered, turned the stove off and sat down to wait with a glass of wine. Ten o'clock passed. Eleven. She tried him again and got his voice mail. Surely if there had been some sort of emergency he would have called?

Eyes burning, head throbbing, she went into the kitchen, dumped dinner into the garbage and brushed her teeth. Told herself to stay calm, that there must be some explanation for this. People didn't just walk out on you.

When she came out of the bathroom, her phone was beeping. She snatched it up and pulled up the text message. It was from Matteo.

Saw you called. Can't talk now. I need to talk to you before the pitch tomorrow. I'll pick you up for a coffee before?

She stared at the message. For a good two or three minutes she just stared at it. Then it hit her. He was dumping her. He was about to accomplish his goal of winning the Luxe contract, so why keep her around any longer? It was just like it had been with Julian. Once she'd outlived her usefulness to him, once he'd forged the contacts he'd needed to with the Davis elite, he'd left.

But why now? Why hadn't he just waited until the pitch was over? Had the guilt gotten to him?

She turned off the lights and slipped into bed. Tears slid down her face—hot, silent. She didn't understand any of it. Didn't understand how her emotions, her instincts could be so wrong.

But she would not let another man break her. She was stronger than that. It's just that she should have known. She really should have known.

CHAPTER FIFTEEN

LIGHT FILTERED THROUGH the floor-to-ceiling windows of Quinn's bedroom, ushering in a new day. Head throbbing, she swiped at her alarm, rolled out of bed and stumbled to the bathroom for a shower. The thought of walking into that pitch room made her feel ill. The coffee with Matteo more so. If he dumped her today, she wasn't sure she was ever going to trust herself again. She had been so sure he was the one.

She pushed shampoo through her hair. Tried to jolt her brain out of the fog it was in. But all she could do was wonder why. What part of her was so deeply bruised, so inherently defective that everyone always left? Her birth parents. Julian. Now Matteo. What was it about her that made them change their minds?

She rinsed her hair, dried herself off and walked into the bedroom, stumbling over the clothes she'd kicked off last night. Her brain on automatic pilot, she stopped in front of the dresser and reached for underwear. Froze at the glint of metal on the top of the dresser.

Matteo's watch. Her heart jumped. *He would never leave something with such sentimental value anywhere unless he intended on coming back.*

Her mind whirling, she turned to the closet and pulled out a blouse. Stopped dead in her tracks when she saw Matteo's favorite suit hanging at the end of the row of her clothes. His lucky suit. The suit he'd been going to wear to the pitch.

Something like hope sprang to life inside her.

I am not going anywhere and neither are you. We are going to do this together. Capisce?

She'd believed him when he'd said it. She'd promised to believe in him. So what was she doing? What if she was wrong? What if he hadn't left?

I need to talk to you before the pitch tomorrow... What did that mean?

What if her past was eating her alive?

Wasn't it time she started believing in something?

Matteo entered the boardroom on the fifty-fifth floor of Davis Investments ten minutes late from a delayed landing, with the tense stance of a man ready to do battle. He was poised to annihilate the past. To right everything that had been wrong and secure his future with Quinn.

He had gone through the presentation with Gabe. It was perfect. He had spent the flight back imprinting every detail on his brain so he could focus on selling it. If this didn't win it for De Campo, nothing would.

Adrenaline firing through him, determination tightening every muscle with purpose, he greeted Walter Driscoll, Luxe's COO and the new head of the decision committee. Shook hands with the others, including Margarite and Warren Davis. It wasn't until he stopped to press a kiss to Quinn's cheek that he noticed she was all wrong. There were big dark bags under her eyes, they were puffy as if she'd been crying and her gaze was so packed full of emotion, he didn't know which one to choose.

"What's wrong?"

Her gaze fell away from his. "Daniel Williams is right after you. You should get started."

He stepped closer. "Quinn, what's wrong?"

She shook her head. Stepped back. "You should start."

He walked to the front of the room, pushed a button on his laptop to project his presentation on to the screen and tried to ignore how the woman he was now convinced he loved beyond a shadow of a doubt looked as if she might cave in at any minute.

Walter Driscoll nodded for him to start. He began, training his gaze on the first slide. Channeling the mood he wanted to create. Focusing on the presentation he could not lose. Heads were nodding, eyes flashing with the recognition of what De Campo could bring to the table as he worked through it—the wines, the restaurant experience, the revolutionary work Gabe was doing in Napa. But the further he got into the presentation, the farther Quinn slid down into her chair, as if it were physically painful for her to be sitting there.

Something inside him snapped. He clicked to the next section of the PowerPoint and set the remote down. "Would you mind," he asked Walter, "if I borrowed Quinn for a moment?"

Walter frowned. "You have fifteen minutes left to make your case, Mr. De Campo. Use them as you will."

Matteo inclined his head toward Quinn whose eyes were as big as saucers. "Join me in the hallway for a moment?"

She started to protest, then a quick glance around the room at the undivided attention the two of them were generating brought her scrambling to her feet. "What are you doing?" she hissed as they walked out into the hallway and he shut the door. "You have at least a third of your presentation left."

He braced his palm against the wall. "Tell me what's wrong."

"Matteo, you need to get back in there and—"

"Not until you tell me why you look like crap."

"Where were you?"

His gaze sharpened. "In California with Gabe like my text said."

She stared at him. "The only text I got was the one that said we needed to talk."

He frowned. "I sent one in the morning before I left. Told you I'd be back today in time for the pitch."

"I never got it."

His mind whirled in a race against time. "Where did you think I was?"

"I thought you'd left."

"Left?"

She squeezed her eyes shut and leaned back against the wall. "The first I knew my marriage had ended was when Julian sent movers on a Saturday morning when he was supposed to be in Boston watching a ball game."

His jaw dropped. "You think I would have walked out like that? Dammit, Quinn, has this week not convinced you of how I feel? I was talking about buying houses with you, for God's sake."

She pressed her palms to her face. "I came home so excited to cook a meal for you. I was so hurt when you weren't there. I didn't get that text. I wasn't thinking rationally. All your things were gone. Then I saw Giancarlo's watch this morning, and your suit, and I told myself I needed to trust you. That for once I needed to have faith in someone." She locked her gaze on his. "Because if it isn't you, Matteo, I won't ever have it."

His heart contracted into a tight fist in his chest. "Do you think a confirmed bachelor starts making plans to buy a house with a woman he isn't crazy about?"

"You were very casual about it."

"I was fishing. Seeing what you thought."

"Oh." A tiny smile curved her lips. "Sometimes I'm not so good at the subtle."

"You don't say." He shook his head. "You operate with all the subtlety of an 18-wheeler."

The vulnerability staining her green eyes tore at his heart. He uttered a low curse. "You are killing me right now, Quinn. I have a very beautiful, very *you* rock in my pocket I was going to give to you in a very romantic proposal after this presentation to prove I love you no matter what happens with this deal. Do *not* make me do this now."

Her eyes rounded. "You have a ring in your pocket?"

"Yes." He put her away from him with a grimace. "Now if you could please wipe the thought from your head, preferably until tonight when I can do it right, I will go and try to secure our future with the ten minutes I have left."

"I'm not sure I can do that," she whispered.

"Work it out," he came back grimly.

She followed him back into the room. Heart racing, he tore ruthlessly through the rest of the presentation in just enough time to get to the last slide, take five minutes of questions and look around the room. All the committee members were smiling except for the cagey Luxe head chef. He exhaled deeply. He'd done all he could. And when it came down to it that's all a man could do. Lay down your best and hope it was enough.

Walter Driscoll thanked him and said he'd be in touch within the week. Matteo shook hands with the others, gathered his things and gave Quinn a pointed look. "Time for a coffee?"

Quinn tried not to think about the ring as she dropped her things off in her office and rode the elevator to the ground floor with Matteo. But she was walking on air and dammit, the man she was crazy about had a ring in his pocket. How was she supposed to pretend it didn't exist?

Her heels clicked on the pavement as they walked outside, her love for this man bigger than all of it. Bigger than the vibrant city that pulsed around them. Bigger than the sunshine beating down on their shoulders, gilding everything in a warm golden glow.

Bigger than the pain of the past.

She tugged on his hand as he dragged her toward the coffee shop on the corner and dug in her heels.

"I can't."

He eyed her. "Can't what?"

She pulled in a breath. "I can't go for a coffee with you when I know you have a ring in your pocket. It is physically impossible."

He lifted a brow. "And what would you have me do? Give it to you now?"

Her lips curved. "Yes."

"You really want to ruin the proposal I had planned?"

"Yes." *Definitively yes.*

All the blood seemed to rush from her head as he reached into his jacket pocket and pulled out a box. And there on Michigan Avenue, one of Chicago's busiest streets, with people streaming by in all directions, he got down on one knee.

A woman walked by, openly ogling the beautiful, charismatic man at her feet, and yes, he was that; yes, he was gorgeous and one of the world's most notorious playboys, but he was so much more than that. He was brilliant in so many different ways he made Quinn's head spin. He was also deep, a philosopher beyond his years and he'd shown her who she truly was.

She was not Quinn the ice queen. She was a woman capable of loving this man with everything she had.

Her heart tattooed itself across her chest, beating a frantic dance as he opened the box to reveal a jaw-droppingly beautiful square-cut emerald surrounded by a band of sparkling white diamonds.

"Your eyes," he said simply. "When they're spitting fire at me, they're the most gorgeous thing I've ever seen."

A little old lady and her husband started to skirt around them. Then she pulled to a halt, her eyes widening. "Look, he's proposing."

Her husband tugged on her arm. "So let him. They don't need an audience."

"They're standing on Michigan Avenue, aren't they?" The blue-haired old lady stood to the side and crossed her arms over her chest. "You just keep going." She nodded to Matteo. "Don't mind us."

Matteo grimaced up at Quinn. "Nice idea of yours, this one."

"Just spit it out," she returned, a smile stretching her lips. "You're used to an audience aren't you?"

"You," he murmured meaningfully, as more people stopped and joined the old couple, "will pay for that later."

Her smile grew even bigger. He took her hand in his. Her eyes widened. Mr. Cool and Collected, who had just put in a rock solid performance under immense pressure the likes of which most men would have buckled underneath, was nervous. The tremor in his strong hand holding hers was enough to make her want to melt to the pavement.

His gaze held hers. "I had no idea what I was looking for until I met you," he said quietly. "I was so lost I didn't know how to find my way back. And you—you have given me clarity in a way I never thought possible, Quinn Davis. You've made me see the man I want to be. How the mistakes I've made have shaped me into who I am." His fingers tightened around hers. "So no matter what happens with this pitch, I have already won the biggest prize."

Her need for air came out as a sob.

"Marry me," he murmured. "Marry me so we can spend the rest of our lives together."

Another sob filled the air, this time from an anonymous woman burying her head in a hankie.

Quinn focused on Matteo. "You make me believe I can do anything. That anything is possible. You make me so much better than I am."

"That's impossible," he said softly, "because you are perfect to me."

A lone tear blazed a trail of fire down her cheek. "I love you."

His gray eyes darkened. "Me, too, *tesoro*. Now give me an answer before this turns into any more of a public spectacle."

"Yes." The word came out more as a croak than an answer, but he got the message and slid the ring on her finger.

"You see," the old lady murmured, "that's how it's done."

The crowd broke out into applause, whistling their approval as Matteo stood and pulled her into his arms.

"I suppose she wants a Hollywood-style kiss," he murmured.

"Undoubtedly." Quinn shot a sideways look at the local news photographer who'd arrived just in time to capture the action. "But after this you're announcing your official magazine-cover retirement."

"I'm good with that." He took her mouth in a kiss that was front-page-worthy and then some. Then he whisked her off on the De Campo jet for the champagne celebration Lilly had planned in New York—the one part of his proposal Quinn hadn't managed to upend.

Lilly and Alex whisked Quinn off when they arrived in the garden, lit with lanterns on a sultry New York summer evening. Riccardo poured the men a scotch. "You know I hate this stuff," Matteo muttered, wrapping his fingers around the glass.

"Be a man," Riccardo taunted. "Walter Driscoll just called. Said he'd been trying to reach you."

Matteo froze. "Have they made a choice?"

"*Si.*" His elder brother swirled the amber liquid around the base of the crystal tumbler. "Want to know?"

His heart stalled in his chest. "Dammit. Do not play with me, Riccardo."

A wide smile split his elder brother's harshly carved face. "You did it, *fratello*. The Luxe contract is ours."

He felt the ground sway under his feet. Three years he had worked to put the past behind him. And just like that, it was done.

"Driscoll said you were brilliant." Something like pride glittered in Riccardo's eyes. "That you made it impossible for them to choose anyone else."

Matteo's heart jump started again. "So we're even then?"

His brother inclined his head. "You were right. I should have let you do it your way." He paused. "Maybe that's the way I should have played it from the start."

"And upset your idea of how the world should be?" Matteo lifted a brow. "Surely not, oh, powerful one."

Riccardo smiled and nodded toward Quinn. "You didn't waste any time putting a ring on her finger. She must be good in bed."

Matteo's fist was cocked and ready to strike when his brother held his up his hand, laughing. "Mine was, too. She was also a hell of a lot more than that. Really, Matty, when are you going to learn I'm just pulling your strings?"

Matteo lowered his fist and scowled. "Maybe if you chose your moments with a bit more finesse…"

"What fun would that be?"

Matteo went off to join his fiancée rather than spar with Riccardo. "Where is buffer brother?" he asked Alex. "He's needed. Badly."

"Getting us something to drink." She jabbed him in the ribs. "Nice work on the photo. It was drop-dead fantastically romantic, Matty. Phone's been ringing off the hook."

They could all wait. He drank his fill of his ridiculously beautiful soon-to-be wife in the cherry-red cocktail dress she wore. It fit perfectly with the third part of his proposal plan that included Quinn alone in his rose-strewn loft Lilly and Alex had done up, with her wearing the ring and nothing else.

Quinn flushed, as if she knew exactly where his head was. "He has a way with words. I think the little old lady watching would have dumped her husband for him."

Gabe came outside, a bottle in his hand. "Congratulations," he murmured, giving Matteo a hug. "I heard the news."

Silence fell over the group. Lilly gave Gabe an expectant look. "I think we should do the toast."

Gabe handed Matteo the bottle. He felt the blood drain from his face as he read the label. *Bianco Frizzante Giancarlo.*

"You finished it," he said slowly, his fingers caressing the elegant slim cylinder.

Gabe nodded. "It's magnificent."

Matteo blinked back the moisture that stung his eyes, his heart feeling too big for his chest. "I need a moment."

He walked to the side of the terrace and looked out over Lilly's wildflower garden. The wine had been his and Gabe's tribute to Giancarlo. They had created it together. But to open it meant acknowledging his friend was gone. To finally let him go.

He wasn't sure he could do it.

Quinn appeared at his side. Took his hand in hers, pried his fingers open and wrapped hers around them. "You loved him, Matteo. This is such a beautiful thing you and Gabe have done for him. Open it and let him go."

His fingers tightened around hers. She was right. It was time. And he could let go, he realized, because Quinn was his future.

They walked back to the others. Gabe uncorked the wine and poured them all a glass. Matteo lifted his. "To my past, to my brother, Giancarlo, who will always be with me." He swallowed past the thickness in his throat. "This one is for you."

The wine tasted fruity and life-affirming on his tongue. *Perfetto.*

He shifted his gaze to the woman at his side. "And to my future. The woman I want to spend the rest of my life with. *Tu sei il mio cuore.*" He leaned down to kiss her. "You are my heart, Quinn Davis."

She gave him a misty-eyed smile. "Really, Matteo De Campo. You are much too silver-tongued."

But she kissed him anyway, her lips clinging to his in a promise of forever. Because for him and Quinn, the journey was just beginning.

* * * * *

Mills & Boon® Hardback
May 2014

ROMANCE

The Only Woman to Defy Him	Carol Marinelli
Secrets of a Ruthless Tycoon	Cathy Williams
Gambling with the Crown	Lynn Raye Harris
The Forbidden Touch of Sanguardo	Julia James
One Night to Risk it All	Maisey Yates
A Clash with Cannavaro	Elizabeth Power
The Truth About De Campo	Jennifer Hayward
Sheikh's Scandal	Lucy Monroe
Beach Bar Baby	Heidi Rice
Sex, Lies & Her Impossible Boss	Jennifer Rae
Lessons in Rule-Breaking	Christy McKellen
Twelve Hours of Temptation	Shoma Narayanan
Expecting the Prince's Baby	Rebecca Winters
The Millionaire's Homecoming	Cara Colter
The Heir of the Castle	Scarlet Wilson
Swept Away by the Tycoon	Barbara Wallace
Return of Dr Maguire	Judy Campbell
Heatherdale's Shy Nurse	Abigail Gordon

MEDICAL

200 Harley Street: The Proud Italian	Alison Roberts
200 Harley Street: American Surgeon in London	Lynne Marshall
A Mother's Secret	Scarlet Wilson
Saving His Little Miracle	Jennifer Taylor

Mills & Boon® Large Print
May 2014

ROMANCE

The Dimitrakos Proposition	Lynne Graham
His Temporary Mistress	Cathy Williams
A Man Without Mercy	Miranda Lee
The Flaw in His Diamond	Susan Stephens
Forged in the Desert Heat	Maisey Yates
The Tycoon's Delicious Distraction	Maggie Cox
A Deal with Benefits	Susanna Carr
Mr (Not Quite) Perfect	Jessica Hart
English Girl in New York	Scarlet Wilson
The Greek's Tiny Miracle	Rebecca Winters
The Final Falcon Says I Do	Lucy Gordon

HISTORICAL

From Ruin to Riches	Louise Allen
Protected by the Major	Anne Herries
Secrets of a Gentleman Escort	Bronwyn Scott
Unveiling Lady Clare	Carol Townend
A Marriage of Notoriety	Diane Gaston

MEDICAL

Gold Coast Angels: Bundle of Trouble	Fiona Lowe
Gold Coast Angels: How to Resist Temptation	Amy Andrews
Her Firefighter Under the Mistletoe	Scarlet Wilson
Snowbound with Dr Delectable	Susan Carlisle
Her Real Family Christmas	Kate Hardy
Christmas Eve Delivery	Connie Cox

Mills & Boon® Hardback
June 2014

ROMANCE

Ravelli's Defiant Bride	Lynne Graham
When Da Silva Breaks the Rules	Abby Green
The Heartbreaker Prince	Kim Lawrence
The Man She Can't Forget	Maggie Cox
A Question of Honour	Kate Walker
What the Greek Can't Resist	Maya Blake
An Heir to Bind Them	Dani Collins
Playboy's Lesson	Melanie Milburne
Don't Tell the Wedding Planner	Aimee Carson
The Best Man for the Job	Lucy King
Falling for Her Rival	Jackie Braun
More than a Fling?	Joss Wood
Becoming the Prince's Wife	Rebecca Winters
Nine Months to Change His Life	Marion Lennox
Taming Her Italian Boss	Fiona Harper
Summer with the Millionaire	Jessica Gilmore
Back in Her Husband's Arms	Susanne Hampton
Wedding at Sunday Creek	Leah Martyn

MEDICAL

200 Harley Street: The Soldier Prince	Kate Hardy
200 Harley Street: The Enigmatic Surgeon	Annie Claydon
A Father for Her Baby	Sue MacKay
The Midwife's Son	Sue MacKay

Mills & Boon® Large Print
June 2014

ROMANCE

A Bargain with the Enemy	Carole Mortimer
A Secret Until Now	Kim Lawrence
Shamed in the Sands	Sharon Kendrick
Seduction Never Lies	Sara Craven
When Falcone's World Stops Turning	Abby Green
Securing the Greek's Legacy	Julia James
An Exquisite Challenge	Jennifer Hayward
Trouble on Her Doorstep	Nina Harrington
Heiress on the Run	Sophie Pembroke
The Summer They Never Forgot	Kandy Shepherd
Daring to Trust the Boss	Susan Meier

HISTORICAL

Portrait of a Scandal	Annie Burrows
Drawn to Lord Ravenscar	Anne Herries
Lady Beneath the Veil	Sarah Mallory
To Tempt a Viking	Michelle Willingham
Mistress Masquerade	Juliet Landon

MEDICAL

From Venice with Love	Alison Roberts
Christmas with Her Ex	Fiona McArthur
After the Christmas Party...	Janice Lynn
Her Mistletoe Wish	Lucy Clark
Date with a Surgeon Prince	Meredith Webber
Once Upon a Christmas Night...	Annie Claydon

0514 GEN STD LP